# BAD, MEMORY, ALBUM

## JOANNA CAMPBELL SLAN

spot on publishing

# CONTENTS

*To All My Readers –*

*When I began this series, I had no idea how many wonderful people I would meet through Kiki. Thank you, thank you, thank you. You mean the world to me!*

*Your friend,*

*Joanna*

**Note:** *In the timeline of Kiki's life, this book comes after **Love, Die, Neighbor** (The Prequel to the Kiki Lowenstein Mystery Series) and before **Paper, Scissors, Death** (Book #1 in the Kiki Lowenstein Mystery Series).*

# 1

———

*M*y husband, George Lowenstein, shook his car keys at me from across the kitchen. My husband is 5'10" with denim blue eyes. In the summer, when he golfs every week, his hair bleaches out to a dark gold color. In many ways, our daughter takes after him, especially with her own blue eyes. "Don't wait up. I'll be home late."

I bit my lower lip rather than blurt out, "You've been gone every night this week." However, even though I said nothing, the accusation in my eyes gave him pause, however. His face colored slightly with embarrassment.

"I, uh, Bill and I have a business meeting with a client."

*Right.* I wondered if his partner, Bill Ballard, was as busy every evening as George was.

It was a Friday night. We'd just lit the Shabbas candles and eaten a quick dinner. My husband had been unusually quiet. After the meal, he had changed out of his suit. Now he was dressed in sharply creased black slacks, a black turtleneck, and a black leather jacket. The cologne that spiced the air was not his daily brand. Instead, it came from a bottle he kept tucked away at the back of the medicine cabinet. The label said Versace. I'm not sure how to pronounce that, which is a big clue that it's very expensive.

I know, and George knows, that the meeting he's attending will include other women. That's the only reason he would splash on his expensive cologne. Men don't care about how each other smell.

Business meeting? *Monkey* business perhaps. While he's out going out on the town with other people, I'm supposed to sit home and twiddle my thumbs.

"Why don't you call a friend? Have a girls only night? Watch a sappy movie?"

"In case you haven't noticed, it's last minute, George. All my friends have plans." Although I used the word "all," what I really meant was "both." I only have two friends in this world: Our cleaning lady, Mert Chambers, and a woman I met in Jazzercise but haven't seen in forever, Maggie Earhart.

"You know how it goes with clients. I have to do what they want on their schedule."

We both knew he was telling a whopper of a lie. A part of me wanted to throw up my hands and say, "Why can't you be just honest? Tell me that you're seeing someone? Isn't it exhausting to pretend you aren't? It's not like you're fooling me!"

I'm not courageous enough to take the wraps off the sad mess that's our marriage. I knew from the start that George married me out of obligation, not love. He's basically a good, decent man, and he has always been kind to me. Maybe that's enough. Maybe I'm silly to ask for more.

I'm sure a lot of women envy me. George has a sort of boyish good looks, and he keeps himself in shape. He dresses nicely, has good manners, and is intelligent. In other words, he's a catch. No one ever expected him to grab onto my hook and get hauled out of the water.

He says that he loves me. What he really means is that he loves me because I'm the mother of his child. Other than that, I am nothing to him. Nothing. Nothing at all.

Anya came racing in from the great room where she'd been curled up on the futon, watching TV. "Daddy, can you take me to Gran's house? She said I could stay over if I wanted. We want to go shopping tomorrow."

George looked to me for an answer.

If Anya left for her grandmother's house, I'd be all alone. I considered asking her to stay, but hanging out with me would be a poor substitute to walking around the mall and spending her grandmother's money.

"Kiki?" George nudged me toward a decision.

Sensing hesitation and a chance to divide and conquer, Anya threw her arms around him. "Huh, Dad, can I? Please? At least I'll get to ride with you since you have to go to a meeting. Please? Please?" Her grip was tight enough to wrinkle his shirt sleeve.

Lately my daughter has been clingy. She's been especially restless when her father goes out at night. It's getting worse and worse because George has been spending more and more time away from home in the evenings.

That, however, is a conversation for another day.

"Hmmm?" George looked to me for a decision. "I'm happy to drop Anya off at Mom's house. If that's okay with you. I mean, if Anya and Mom are planning to go shopping...uh...unless you'd like to take Anya? Maybe you'd like to go shopping with my mother, too?"

*Don't make me laugh,* I thought to myself. *It'll be a cold day in Miami when Sheila Lowenstein and I go shopping together.*

I made one half-hearted attempt to keep my daughter at home. "Anya, didn't you and your grandmother go shopping a couple of weeks ago? Is there anything in particular you need?"

Anya raised denim blue eyes to me, and her gaze held a hint of embarrassment. "Yeah, we did, but Gran says I need something to wear for homecoming. She says everyone at CALA dresses up, and she wants me to fit in. She wants me to look like I belong and not like I'm trailer trash."

The words came as a slap in my face, as Sheila had known they would. On her insistence, we agreed to send Anya to CALA, the Charles and Anne Lindbergh Academy, a hoity-toity private school that generations of Lowensteins had attended. From the day Anya was born, Sheila raved about the school. Whenever possible, and often when not appropriate, she talked disparagingly about public schools. Her comments made it clear this was not only about the quality of education. It was also about the quality of people in those two settings.

"Trailer trash," I repeated.

George coughed and became intensely interested in the crown molding. He looked everywhere but at me. He knew and I knew that "trailer trash" was Sheila's newest way of putting me down. His mother had made no secret of the fact that she hadn't wanted George to marry me. As punishment, she specialized in little jabs designed to make me feel insecure.

At the same time, she adored her grandchild. Sheila would do anything to make Anya happy. Anything. While I tired of her patrician attitude, I appreciated the fact she strove to give Anya the finer things of life.

Mustering up a smile, I said, "We certainly wouldn't want you to look like trailer trash, would we? If Sheila says that everyone at CALA dresses up for homecoming, then it must be true. Besides, no one at the Charles and Anne Lindbergh Academy does anything by halves, do they? Come here. Give me a hug and a kiss. Good girl. Grab your jacket."

Luckily, Anya ignored my thinly veiled sarcasm and raced to the hall closet.

"Sorry," George mumbled under his breath.

Anya came back with one arm inside a sleeve and the other searching for the armhole. "What'll you do while we're gone, Mom?"

"Drink champagne and eat bonbons."

"Your mom is so funny." George stepped in and guided Anya's hand into her coat sleeve. Turning to me, he asked, "You didn't forget that we have Lily Grey, the interior designer, coming to the house on Monday, did you?"

Interior designer? He must mean the interior decorator. I didn't challenge the terminology he used. George was usually right about such things.

"Lily's fitting us in as a special favor. Normally, she doesn't have time for small jobs like this."

Small jobs like this? We had four thousand square feet, not counting the finished basement. In what world was that a small job? Leave it to Lily to suggest she was doing us a favor. I remembered how condescending she had been when she picked out the tile, the fixtures, the finishes, the baseboard, and the colors of the exterior. I acquiesced to her choices because as George reminded me, she's an expert, and I'm not. Part of my reason was practical. When you're making selections for a house this big, a wrong choice can be really expensive.

After we moved in, I had hoped to decorate our home myself. However, George had strong opinions about what was appropriate. "This place needs to look fashionable and elegant. Our house has to announce to the world that I'm successful. On my way up in the world."

Silly me. I'd thought our home should be a comfortable, inviting living space.

Each time I found a piece I liked George hesitated. He didn't say no. He didn't say yes. He simply procrastinated.

Recently, his mother began to make snide comments like, "Love what you've done with the place."

Not surprisingly, George had arranged for Lily Grey to decorate our home from floor to ceiling. I had a hunch that Lily hoped I would stand aside and watch. Sheila had let it slip that Lily expected that a glossy St. Louis magazine would do a feature on our house. A feature designed to showcase "her" talents.

We were the lucky dogs who'd get to pick up the bill. Once Lily was gone, we'd be stuck living with whatever she chose, even if her décor did not mesh with our preferences. Correction: *my* preferences.

I wasn't willing to step aside. "George, you promised me that Lily will include me in the decision making. Please warn her in advance that I want to have input."

George twirled his car keys around his index finger.

"Well," he drew that word out.

I knew that tone. It was his, "I don't want to be pinned down" voice.

Clearing his throat, he seemed to gather his self-confidence. "Of course, she'll listen. I'm sure she will. But don't forget, that she is the professional here, right? It doesn't make much sense to pay her for her time and then ignore her advice, does it? You need to remember that she's done work for all the best homes in St. Louis. I had a tough time getting her to fit us into her calendar. Everyone speaks so highly of Lily's talent."

Cue the underlying message: You, Kiki, were born missing any semblance of good taste. We all agree to that.

All these thoughts raced through my mind, and they must have shown up on my face as well.

"Now, Kiki," said George in his best cajoling tones. "Don't get that look on your face. This'll be fun. You filled out those forms for her, right? If you want her to consider your ideas, you will need to be prepared. Do you have a file of pictures? Pages torn from magazines?"

*Right.* I could just imagine that Lily Grey was going go wild over my trailer trash ideas on decorating.

Anya tugged on her father's arm. "Let's get going."

"Gotta run." George gave me an obligatory peck on the cheek. "Meet you in the car, Anya. Tell your mother goodbye."

I grabbed Anya for a quick hug. "Be good for your grandmother."

Anya laughed. "What you really need, Mom, is a hobby."

"Uh-huh," I said. "That's probably true."

With that she skipped away from me. I followed her to the door and watched as she slid into the passenger seat of her dad's black Mercedes convertible. After she glanced down to find both ends of her seatbelt, she gave me a little wave goodbye.

Only after I heard the garage door roll shut did I realize that I'd been duped. Instead of grilling George on where he was going this evening or why he was having so many late meetings recently, I'd gotten drawn into a conversation about Lily Grey.

I felt more lonely than ever.

George and I both were making the best of a bad situation. He'd never intended to marry me, and I'd never planned on marrying him. We were brought together by an overindulgence, too much spiked punch at a frat party. My first experience with sex was certainly memorable. I guess you could say I was a "one and done" type of girl, because I immediately became pregnant. George only married me because he's a stand-up guy who wanted to do the right thing. Even though we barely knew each other, we agreed that family comes first. Anya is the center of our relationship. We make all our decisions after considering what's best for her.

To my credit, that's exactly what I'd had on my mind when I'd dropped out of college. At first, I thought I might be able to keep attending classes, but the intensity of my morning sickness made that impossible.

George was very kind and very understanding.

"You can always go back later," he said.

"Right." I agreed in principle, but in my heart of hearts, I thought that returning to college was highly unlikely. Growing up, I'd done a lot of babysitting. I knew how busy mothers could get. Sure, it depended a lot on the baby, but even with the happiest infants, the mothers I saw were often exhausted. While George approached parenthood with starry eyes, I had both feet on terra firma.

Of course, I hadn't factored in the nearly immediate death of Harry Lowenstein, my father-in-law. Nor could I have guessed at how that death would shape our family dynamics.

Without Harry, his wife Sheila was adrift and George was stunned. The old man had clearly been the rock on which the family had been built. George put on a good face at the funeral, but Sheila fell apart. She didn't cry. She simply went blank like a TV that's on the fritz. Holding onto George's arm as we left the temple, she shuffled her feet like a zombie in a bad B movie. Standing at the graveside, George had to put the dirt in her hand and help her toss it into the hole so that it landed on top of the coffin. We braced her like a pair of bookends and marched her back to the black limousine. During *shiva,* the traditional seven days of mourning, she was dressed and groomed by Linnea, the Lowenstein family maid. Linnea reported that Sheila quit eating and would have gladly stayed in bed all day. Most shocking of all, Sheila neglected her appearance. George and I both worried over her mental health. I shudder to think what she might have done to herself if she hadn't had Anya, her one and only grandchild.

One day, two months after Harry's death, Sheila rose like the mythical phoenix. To this day, I have no idea what reinvigorated her. All I know is that she got out of bed, put on her makeup, and resumed her rightful spot as Queen of Everything. That includes the role as Grandmother of the Century.

My mother-in-law clearly adores Anya and willingly watches her. On the minus side, Sheila makes impossible demands. She has high standards for housekeeping, she is a social butterfly who regularly obligates us to events, and she is a devoted philanthropist who expects us to give of our time to various causes. In addition, our presence is expected several times a week at the Lowenstein family home off of Litzsinger, one of the better addresses in the metro St. Louis area.

You'd think with school, temple, and the weekly visits to my mother-in-law's house, I'd never be lonely, and you'd be wrong. Sheila has a way of sucking the oxygen out of a room. George does fine when she's around, but I trail the Lowenstein duo like a bad smell. I am not confident enough to make my presence known. To be totally honest, I suspect that Sheila enjoys the attention of her admiring son while rubbing it in that I am not Miss Popularity.

Alone in my laundry room, as I folded sheets warm from the dryer, I reminded myself that even if Sheila is a pill, my daughter benefits from her grandmother's involvement. Thanks to Sheila's connections, George heard about a vacant lot we bought at a steal, which allowed us to build a honking big house in a ritzy St. Louis suburb, Ladue. Thanks to Sheila's networking in the business community, George has gotten several leads that had given his fledgling business a real boost. Doors open for George and Anya because of Sheila. She is unstoppable when it comes to getting whatever she wants for herself or those she loves.

I feel a tad jealous of my husband. I've never had the sort of support his parents gave him. My mother is not the president of my personal fan club. My dad is dead. When he was alive, he ran a reign of terror with his violent outbursts and nasty tongue. All of us were afraid of him.

My two sisters are younger than I. I communicate rarely with Amanda, who lives in Arizona with my mother. Catherine is estranged, and I haven't heard from her in years. The closest I have to a supportive relative is my Aunt Penny, a woman who isn't really blood kin at all, but a friend from my mother's brief college career.

The sad truth of the matter is that I'd entered this marriage on an unequal footing with George. After saying, "I do," my stock plummeted significantly. When we'd met, I was a journalism major, a college student with an A average. Now I am a drop-out, a mom, and a drudge.

No wonder George doesn't want to spend more time with me. No wonder he doesn't consider me his soulmate. Obviously, I am not the love of his life.

To be perfectly honest, I'm the person who has the most to lose if our marriage hit the rocks. George could survive a divorce, but I can't say the same. Not at all. The disparity I'd felt when we first married has only grown bigger as the years rolled along. My husband completed his college classes and got his degree. He and his partner, Bill Ballard, have their own venture, Dimont Development. George is quickly building a good reputation in his industry.

I have nowhere to go. No resources. No education. No family who would take me in or offer assistance. As for an employment history, all I have on my resume are a few skimpy babysitting jobs from my teenage years.

I could probably find work with Mert, our cleaning lady, but I certainly couldn't make enough money to support Anya in the way she lives right now. If my marriage collapsed, my daughter would resent the change in her circumstances...if she stayed with me.

If she lived with George...

I couldn't imagine that. It would break my heart.

What I needed was to re-commit myself to my marriage.

"Tons of people have problems with their marriages. That doesn't mean it's a bad marriage. No marriage is perfect," I spoke sternly to myself as I lined up the edges of the towels in the linen closets.

"I need a hobby," I explained to a teetering pile of washcloths right before they tipped over. "I must insist that we develop friends as a couple. I can start by getting this place decorated so we can invite people over for get togethers. That means I better be prepared for when Lily Grey comes to visit."

Not surprisingly, the towels had nothing to say.

## 2

ith Lily's visit in mind, I took a tour of our house, trying to envision how the place might look when it was furnished properly. What we had now was mainly stuff left over from Sheila's garage and George's college apartment. We'd rented a fully furnished apartment when we first got married, and we moved here shortly before Anya turned two. We hadn't accumulated much in the way of worldly goods.

There were three folding chairs, an old recliner, a futon, George's dresser from his childhood, and plastic stackable drawers. At garage sales, I'd picked up two folding card tables. One we used for mealtimes. We'd been sleeping on mattresses on the floor ever since we'd moved. The one big purchase we'd made was a flat screen television. That was definitely not my idea, but my husband had insisted. George's mother had made him a gift of furnishing his home office. Sheila had gone all out, and I have to admit that it's the most beautiful room in our house.

George and I have distinctively different viewpoints when it came to décor. I love old furniture. I love recycling, reusing, and repurposing things. I cherish the stories behind the objects in my life. Old pieces usually came with a provenance or an explanation about how you happened to own them. To me, that's infinitely cool.

George doesn't like anything that's been previously owned. To him, that qualifies as somebody else's junk.

I do agree with George in one aspect. This house is too upscale for casual furnishings. Lily Grey had seen to that. While we were building, she insisted that we put white marble flooring in most of the rooms. I would have preferred wood or wood laminate. Wall-to-wall white marble makes the whole house feel cold to me. It's like living in a mausoleum.

In addition to the chilly vibe, marble is also really slick. You have to be careful if your feet are wet or if your shoes have new soles. Twice now, I've landed on my keister. Rugs would help. Colorful and soft underfoot. I love old hooked rugs, but I can't imagine them in this house.

I wondered how George would explain that he and I sleep in separate rooms, a tradition that started after Anya was born, when he complained about my getting up in the middle of the night to feed her. Since then, we've fallen into the habit of sleeping apart, especially because he's out late so often.

Maybe that needed to change.

I climbed the winding staircase with its carved rosewood handrail. I took a right at the landing, and headed into my bedroom. Although I didn't have furniture, I had boxes. One of them had been carefully labeled, "Magazines." Opening the flaps, I grabbed two issues of *Metropolitan Home*. Scanning one page after the other, I found three pages with room settings that sort of appealed to me.

Not much to go on.

The rest of the magazines I'd collected were all about casual chic, industrial chic, or thrifty decorating. None of that would work here. I added "buy more upscale décor" magazines to my "to do" list.

Downstairs in George's office—the only room in the house with real furniture—I found office materials. I grabbed a cheerful green file folder and pen. Printing neatly, I wrote "Home Décor" on a white sticky label and slapped it down. Then I slipped the three magazine pages inside.

I also wrote my "to do" list on a yellow legal pad. That left me with nothing to do except twiddle my thumbs. Handing Lily a folder with only three pages in it would be tantamount to giving her carte blanche. By doing so, I would forfeit any right to complain about the outcome of her efforts. I needed to stop by Home Depot and get paint samples. Ditto finding more décor magazines to rip apart.

But that wouldn't take much time. What would I do with the rest of my day?

Anya had been right. I needed a hobby. We didn't have any pets, because George thought animals were messy. That's true, but life is messy, isn't it? I had grown up with a beagle, and we'd had cats that lived outdoors but wandered inside to eat. I'd concluded that the chores were well worth the joy of pet owner-ship. However, George had put his foot down.

*What could I do for a hobby? What would I like to do?*

I enjoyed drawing, but I had no idea what to do with my finished pictures.

I liked taking photos. We had boxes of them.

History had always appealed to me.

So did crafts of any sort.

I left George's office and walked to the bookshelves framing the television, which had been mounted over the fireplace. From the far end of one shelf, I pulled a thin book, a fabric scrapbook.

Nana had made this album for me. She'd cut large rectangles of black cotton fabric with pinking shears, and then stitched the sheets together with bright red seam binding tape. This formed an oversized book with fabric pages. Once assembled, she'd glued in colorful images cut from greeting cards and magazines. As I ran a hand over the rough-edged images, I remembered sitting beside my grandmother on her porch swing. She held the fabric album in her lap while we discussed the pictures. We made up stories to go with them.

A lump rose in my throat and a prickling tickled my eyes. Nana had been the light of my life. She'd taught me to sew by hand. Patiently, she'd shown me how to rub thread between my fingertips until it knotted. Together we'd stitched doll clothes. Once my fingers became more nimble, she showed me how to do cross stitch. Indeed, she had cross-stitched my name on the back of my fabric album.

If I was going to do crafts, I wanted to make something similar to this, a piece that evoked warm feelings of love.

A thought came to me, a memory from a recent grocery store visit. While standing in the check-out lane, I'd thumbed through a magazine devoted to something called "modern scrapbooking." Although the examples didn't look much like the book that Nana had made, the idea appealed to me. The editor explained that saving photos wasn't enough. You also needed to tell the stories behind the photos. Otherwise, the pictures were meaningless. On a whim, I'd thrown the magazine into my grocery cart. Where had that publication gone? Surely I hadn't thrown it out.

Looking down at the carefully cut out images Nana had glued to the fabric, I realized that her stories were missing. How I longed to hear her voice or read her words again!

Returning to my bedroom and the open cardboard box, I dug through the assortment of DIY decorating magazines and found the scrapbook magazine at the bottom of the stack. Sitting cross-legged on the floor, I skimmed the publication. What they called "memory albums" seemed like a great way to display pictures I'd been taking. I could write down the stories I remembered from my childhood. I could save the new stories that were happening daily in our lives. I could preserve all this for Anya.

Where could I learn more about this new hobby?

In the back of the scrapbook magazine, there was a store directory. Time in a Bottle, touting itself as the premiere scrapbook store in the metro St. Louis area, wasn't too far from our home. Ripping out that page, I decided to take a drive.

On my way, I stopped by Home Depot. Their colorful display of paint samples made me giddy. I picked two dozen of the color strips I liked best. Next to the samples were brochures, featuring on-trend colors and interior design. One of every design brochure fit neatly in my purse. On my way out the door, I noticed a rack of decorating magazines. Flipping through, I found five that I liked with styles that were more formal than casual. Inwardly, I did a happy dance! Now I would be well-prepared for my visit with Lily.

Back in my car, I drove to the address on the magazine page. It took me to a neighborhood that could best be called transitional. The building numbers jumped around, although I narrowed them down to several spots along a busy north-south road. Counting off the buildings as I drove by, I pegged Time in a Bottle as a brick building, backing up to a residential area that was slowly becoming more and more distressed. Eventually, all these buildings and the houses, too, would probably be torn down. What a shame that would be! Although the buildings themselves were dumpy and old, over the years, owners had planted maples, oaks, and sweetgum trees. The reward was now on full display as trees flared red and yellow and magenta. Smaller shrubs were every bit as colorful, flaming up in rich gold, robust orange, and wine-red burgundy.

If (and when) a developer, such as my husband, got his hands on this block, he would bring in a bulldozer and knock everything to the ground. After he reduced the structures to dust and the plants to twigs, he would pave over the rich dirt with asphalt. As a final decorative touch, he'd order a few young plants to be tucked in, here and there. It would take decades for this little patch of ground to grow anything worth a second look, much less a long, slow stare of appreciation such as I was giving it now.

Sighing, I drove twice around the block, scoping where I might park. Because the name Time in a Bottle could indicate a watch or clock shop, I'd actually driven past this place numerous times without realizing what it was. Now that I knew what sort of merchandise the store carried, the name not only made sense, it also tickled me. I pulled into the parking lot, turned off the engine, and mustered my courage to go inside. Would the sales-people be welcoming or would they laugh at my ignorance?

There was only one way to find out. I forced myself out of the car, and I walked across the pavement to the front door of the store. A door minder buzzed as I stepped inside and came to an abrupt halt. I had entered an Aladdin's Cave, a place of wonders and treasures that sent my senses reeling. On every side of me were wire racks filled with paper of varying colors. A wire display tower could be rotated to show off stickers. Another display unit was packed with paper punches. Next to that was a shelf full of rubber stamps and inks. For a moment I felt dizzy in the midst of all these foreign objects. What did they have to do with scrapbooking? How were you supposed to use them?

"Welcome, I'm Dodie Goldfader," said a deep voice, "and this is my store." Dodie was nearly six feet tall, broad-shouldered, with a gait that could best be described as "lumbering." You'd have to describe her face as plain, but her eyes sparkled with an energy that rendered her coarse features almost pretty.

"Hi." I stood there. I wasn't sure what else to say or do.

"Are you here to sign up for the crop?" Dodie smiled encouragingly.

"Crop?" I knew I needed to get my hair trimmed, but I hadn't expected someone at a scrapbook store to notice my split ends.

"A crop is a scrapbook party. We have one scheduled at six tonight. You are welcome to join us."

This was when the pedal hit the metal, so to speak. Would I really take the plunge?

"Is there a fee? I didn't sign up. You might not have room. I can come back. Another day? Maybe."

Dodie barked a laugh. "There's no fee for your first class. We have room. Why not join us?"

I hesitated. As I did, Dodie stepped closer and gave me an up-and-down examination. "You're Kiki, aren't you? George Lowenstein's wife?"

"Guilty as charged," I blurted out.

My bad attempt at making a joke landed like a water balloon at my feet. Dodie looked momentarily confused before she snickered. "Lucky you. Sheila's your mother-in-law, right?"

"Uh-huh."

From the back of the store another voice sang out, "Did someone say Sheila? As in Sheila Lowenstein?"

A plump woman whose dark brown hair was cut in an appealing shag approached us. She offered me her hand. "I'm Eloise Silverman. I've seen you at temple. That's how Dodie and I know Sheila." Her hazel eyes looked steadily into mine. Although Eloise wasn't a natural beauty, she was well put together. She'd used makeup to subtly highlight her advantages, a nice complexion and lovely arched brows.

"Temple? You've seen me there? I'm new to Judaism. Every visit to temple is a little overwhelming for me. Dodie? You look familiar. But I'm not sure that I've seen you before, Eloise."

Eloise chuckled softly. "Temple is overwhelming? With Sheila Lowenstein at your side, it would be. She can make anything dramatic."

Dodie cleared her throat. A look passed between her and Eloise. I translated it as a warning from Dodie that Eloise should not to disparage my mother-in-law. A part of me was grateful; a competing part would have listened to anyone bad-mouthing Sheila all day long. The fact that other people found my mother-in-law difficult came as a relief.

At least I wasn't going crazy.

"Eloise, you'll be back this evening for the crop, won't you? I thought so. I'm trying to convince Kiki she should come."

"I'll be back. What else would I be doing, Dodie? My only child lives almost nine hundred miles away. My husband ran off without a forwarding address. Except for Polly, my cat, I'm all alone." Eloise ran her hands down the front of her gathered blouse and tugged on the hem. I recognized the gesture. When you're overweight, you spend a lot of time trying to arrange your clothing strategically.

But that didn't make sense. Not really. Eloise wasn't overweight. Yes, she was a bit on the plump side, but pleasingly so. However, she was tall. She actually towered over me. And she was big boned.

Eloise continued, "Yes, that's me, Dodie. A wallflower. All dressed up and nowhere to go. Why did I bother? Why did I work so hard to lose all that weight? What did it get me but grief?"

Dodie grabbed the other woman in a one-arm hug. "You bothered because your life depended on it. Because you promised your daughter, Cynthia, you'd be there for her wedding. You wanted a better life for yourself. It's not your fault Ben didn't understand. Quit beating yourself up, Eloise."

The intimacy of their conversation made me slightly uncomfortable. Clearly, I'd walked in on two friends sharing a deep dark secret.

When Dodie turned loose of the other woman, I saw the silver sparkle of tears in Eloise's eyes. With a sniff, she sleeved them away. "Sure. All those reasons. That's why. But was it the right thing to do?"

"Get ahold of yourself, El. You absolutely did the right thing. In your heart of hearts, you know it. I saw how much pain you were in. I was there when you had to be rushed to the hospital. I visited you when they cut back on your pain meds. Don't listen to what the other women say. You definitely did the right thing. You aren't responsible for them being jealous."

The conversation made me uncomfortable so I hurried over to look at a rack of stickers. That turned my back toward Dodie and Eloise. Short of leaving, and I had just arrived, getting engrossed in something other than their highly charged conversation seemed like the best way to make myself scarce.

I hate it when a conversation goes over my head. George and his mother do this all the time. They'll be talking about something, and I'll be totally in the dark, but they keep going. It's almost like they enjoy knowing I'm on the outside, and they're a tiny club of two. In some ways, this was the same. Neither Eloise nor Dodie offered to clue me in on the backstory.

However, in this case I didn't mind. At least, not much. I caught the drift. Eloise had lost weight and come to regret it. Dodie had seen her struggle, and commended her for the choices she made. They weren't trying to exclude me. They were deeply involved in a highly charged conversation.

Eloise and Dodie chatted quietly for a little longer. Eventually, Eloise walked over and spoke directly to me. "You should plan to join us for a crop, Kiki. It's a great way to get out of the house and spend time with other women. We always have fun at our crops."

She paused and amended her remark. "Well, nearly always."

"I've never done any scrapbooking. Won't I be out of place?"

"*Oy,* a scrapbooking virgin," Dodie teased me as she wandered our way. "Seriously, Sunshine, a crop is as good a way as any to learn the craft."

"Won't I need supplies?" I needed an excuse not to commit. Glancing at all the supplies, I thought I'd found one.

"Not at first. We have everything you need. Come see whether this might be a hobby you'll enjoy before you spend any of your hard-earned cash with me."

I hesitated. Dodie and Eloise stared at me with expectant expressions on their faces.

"Okay," I said. "Sure."

**3**

---

*I* had nearly four hours to kill until the crop. Back in my Lexus SUV, I closed my eyes and flipped through a mental list of things I like to do. In seconds, I seized on the idea of visiting the St. Louis Art Museum. Like many of the attractions in our city, this one is free and first class. Not surprisingly, it's also fabulous. Just flat out freaking fabulous.

At the front of the building is an enormous statue called Apotheosis of St. Louis showing the saint himself on horseback. What tickles me about good old St. Louis is that he never flinches even though he's occasionally hit by errant golf balls because he sits on the edge of the Forest Park Golf Course. Somehow, I don't think that's what the sculptor had in mind when he fitted the armor on this hero.

Inside the art museum is Anya's favorite exhibit, the Egyptian collection of three mummies in glass cases. Using 3-D printing, the museum has been able to reproduce a scarab piece that was buried alongside one of the bodies. As technology improves, the mummies are quietly yielding their secrets while staying "under wraps."

Today I spent extra time wandering the museum hallways and eventually studying a painting by Max Beckmann called "Christ and the Woman Taken in Adultery." The museum actually has at least six pieces that Nazis considered degenerate, and the Beckmann painting is one of them. As I stood there in front of the canvas, I wondered what future generations will define as degenerate art. Seems to me, that's a political term as well as a subjective one.

After milling around for a couple of hours, I went to the museum restaurant and treated myself to a nice meal. With the floor to ceiling glass windows and the Dale Chihuly wine chandelier, the museum restaurant is one of the most appealing eating spots in the city.

By the time I left the St. Louis Art Museum and headed for Time in a Bottle, my emotional batteries had been fully re-charged. As a bonus, if anyone asked, I could sound incredibly sophisticated when I explained how I'd spent my afternoon.

With a spring in my step, I entered Time in a Bottle. Dodie greeted me and walked me toward the back of the store. I was surprised to see that other people had already arrived and gotten down to work.

"Am I late?"

Dodie shook her head. "No. Others showed up early. Glad you came back. Let's find you a seat."

Before she did, one of the women glanced up from her mess and gave me a big grin.

"Kiki? Come sit by me."

Relief washed over me as I took the empty chair next to my pal, Maggie Earhart. I hadn't recognized her because she was wearing a red polo shirt and mom jeans. I gave her a quick hug and hung my purse over the seat next to hers.

"I haven't seen you at Jazzercise in forever," Maggie said.

"Yup. I guess I got out of the habit." I angled myself in my chair so I could watch what she was doing.

Maggie is solid and built like a LEGO block. She dyes her hair at home with varying results. Once it turned out a sort of greenish-brown. Today it was ash blond. I like Maggie. She is practical, down-to-earth, and candid. Since we live at opposite ends of town, I rarely have the chance to spend time with her unless we see each other at Jazzercise. I made a mental note to start going back to classes.

Boy, would George and Anya ever be surprised. I was really taking the "find yourself a hobby" bull by the horns!

Maggie's usual cologne, a strawberry fragrance, lightly scented the air around her. She manipulated paper and tools with surprising proficiency. Obviously, my pal knew exactly what she was doing. I, of course, was clueless. But here we were, side by side at a scrapbook store.

That had to be a good omen, didn't it?

I DID my best to pay attention to names as the other women introduced themselves. Three of them—Karen, Angie, and Mel —acted like best friends. They chatted with each other, sharing supplies and having a terrific time. All three were large women, easily topping three hundred pounds. The fact they were plus-size made me feel right at home. Karen Falk was a redhead with lavish eye makeup. She wore a floral dress over a pair of purple leggings. Her clogs were bright green. Angie Paulson had dark brown hair, cut in a pageboy. Her dark brown eyes sparkled with curiosity directed toward her friends. Her oversized sweatshirt was decorated with a picture of a shy bunny sniffing a flower. Mel Acker was a dishwater blonde, and the largest of the three. She'd cropped her hair into a buzz cut, but her lavish eye makeup and bright red lips offset the severity of her hairstyle with loads of overt femininity. Her peasant-styled, white cotton top was embroidered in a folk art pattern. Clearly, Mel was the leader. The others deferred to her.

The fourth woman at the table was Eloise. She must have arrived shortly before I did. She quickly shot me a smile. "Welcome back."

"Thanks," I said.

There had been an empty chair on each side of Eloise, one between her and Maggie, and one between her and Angie. I had slipped into the chair between Maggie and Eloise. Belatedly, I realized that until I showed up, Eloise had set herself apart from the others with that barrier of chairs. The cautious smile she sent my way suggested she was fine with me encroaching on her space.

By contrast, she would sneak looks at the other three women, being careful not to engage them. Once I got over my awkwardness, I detected a tension in the air that wasn't directed toward me. Out of the corner of my eye, I realized the other three women had turned up their volume a notch. An artificial gaiety blossomed around them. In short, they were having too good of a time, and their fun was on full display. That didn't make sense to me. Why were they going out of their way to act up? It was the type of over-the-top showmanship that you'd see from a group of teenagers at the mall and not from three adult women considerably past the point of needing approval by their peers.

In an unguarded moment, after a particularly loud guffaw from Angie, I saw Dodie frown at the gleesome threesome. Bless my pal Maggie's heart, she kept her head down and concentrated on a stack of photos of her kids at a local apple orchard. After separating out a handful, she planned exactly how to use them.

Ten minutes after the start of the crop, Dodie locked the front door and turned over the CLOSED sign. Once her duties as merchant were concluded, she hurried to my side. Tucked under one arm was a navy blue photo album.

"Okay, Sunshine, let me give you a crash course in what we're doing here." Dodie sat the album in front of me and flipped it open. For the next five minutes while I looked at the pages, she leaned over my shoulder and explained what sat "modern scrapbooking" apart from yesterday's photo albums. "This is all about telling stories. See the writing in my book? That's what we call journaling. I'm actually telling you who's in each picture, what they're doing, and why it matters. Pictures are great, but one day you won't be around to narrate what's happening in the snaps. Your job as a scrapbooker is to capture these stories and preserve them for the next generation."

She was still leaning over me when she added, "A picture is worth a thousand words, but we're all thankful that the Declaration of Independence wasn't a sketch on parchment."

Her pause at that point was longer than I expected. I turned in my seat and looked up at her. To my surprise, she winked. "Of course, having fun while you're doing this is absolutely mandatory. Personally, I doubt that any scrapbooking can get done without copious amounts of food. Ladies, don't you agree?"

Maggie smirked, while Angie and crew nodded vigorously. Eloise wore a wistful smile on her face. She dug into her purse and pulled out three oranges. "These days, I tame my sweet tooth with fruit. Typically, mandarin oranges that I can peel and eat in sections."

"Poor substitute, if you ask me," Angie sniffed. Her friends showed their agreement by waving an assortment of candy bars. "My motto is: Sugar, food of the gods. Don't leave home without it."

"Part of my job is to make sure my scrappers have everything they need to enjoy themselves," Dodie explained to me.

She launched into a long dissertation about why people should use acid-free and archival safe products. Evidently, such products would protect my precious photos. I'd already noticed that many family photos from the 60s and 70s were starting to fade. According to Dodie, this was a devastating combination of bad developing chemicals and poorly sourced albums. In particular, the cameras that offered "instant" photos were to blame. The chemistry behind the quick development of the images was not particularly stable.

It dawned on me that I was woefully unprepared for this excursion. "I didn't bring any photos with me. I wasn't sure what I'd be doing."

"No big deal. Most photos are standard sizes. You can make pages, leave the space open for photos, and fill them in later." Dodie grinned at me. "Make yourself comfortable while I round up supplies for you. Get up and walk around the table if you like. See what everyone else is doing. That'll give you a taste of what a crop is."

Eloise had a variety of photos spread in front of her. Many showed her in a slinky turquoise dress, obviously at a wedding. One showed Eloise adjusting the veil of a bride.

"Is that your daughter? The one who moved away?"

"Yes. My Cindy."

"Looks like her wedding was beautiful. Your dress is gorgeous. You look fabulous."

"Of course, she looked fabulous. That was the plan." Mel raised her head to chime in. Her eyes narrowed to small pinpricks. "Eloise wanted everything to be perfect for Cindy, so she took the easy way out. She had gastric bypass surgery. Lost half her weight."

"Month after month, all she ate three times a day was a hard-boiled egg." Angie glared over at Eloise.

Since I personally don't much care for eggs that sounded like torture to me. I couldn't imagine existing on one egg after another.

"My doctor had made it clear to me. Either I lost the weight or I'd die." Eloise directed her comments toward me, but I knew she was also answering Angie and Mel.

"You say that as if WLS isn't dangerous." Karen crossed her arms over her chest.

"WLS?" I repeated.

"Weight Loss Surgery. Some statistics show that 22% have complications after their surgery," Karen said. "One in every two hundred will die. I'm a nurse. I've seen first-hand how wrong it can go. Gallstones, bowel obstructions, dumping syndrome. And the cost? Eloise could have bought a new car with all the money she spent."

Eloise jutted out her jaw. Her pretty face had turned stone-like with anger. "That was my money. I inherited it from my dad. He wanted me to have the surgery. That's the last thing he said to me before he died. He was worried about my health, and he begged me to do something. He told me to use his insurance money to save my own life."

"Puh-leze." Mel sneered. "You could have gone with us to Weight Watchers. You could have gone on that liquid diet like Angie did. Instead, you took the easy way out. You went under the knife for instant results. Then you dumped us."

"I did no such thing. You three made it clear you don't approve of what I've done. You don't want me around."

"Blah-blah-blah." Mel waved her hand in a lazy circle. "We aren't good enough for you anymore."

The conversation made me uncomfortable. I couldn't imagine surgery as ever being an easy way out. Things could go so horribly, terribly wrong.

Eager to change the subject, I moved from Eloise to Karen. She was making a page about a visit to her hair stylist. The two had discussed what color would be best for Karen because over the years her coloring had changed slightly. A few stray gray hairs had crept into her tresses, making her feel older than she was. Working with the stylist, she picked a new shade of red that seemed to suit her down to the ground.

"That's quite a transformation." I pointed at her before and after photos. The red coloring lit up her face and brought attention to her creamy skin.

Karen smiled up at me. "I guess, but it wasn't expensive. Not really. I went while the salon was having a special, and I took advantage of their sale to have a complete make-over."

"The results are amazing." I couldn't believe the photos illustrated the same woman.

Angie leveled a look at me. "Karen was very careful with her money. She didn't blow it. Good old Eloise raced through $15,000 for her surgery and another grand working with a stylist who really went to town, dolling her up. After they changed the color, Eloise went and had hair extensions put in. She got false eyelashes. A professional did her makeup, and then taught her how to use everything. Of course, she looked fabulous when it all was finished. Eloise spent tons of money."

Angie snorted, a terribly un-ladylike sound that shocked me. "That's nothing compared to what Eloise spent getting that excess skin taken off."

I could feel the color start at the base of my throat and slowly rise until it scorched my cheeks. This conversation had turned intensely personal and critical. Here I'd thought scrapbooking would offer a good time! Instead, I was listening to a laundry list of Eloise Silverman's mistakes.

Dodie must have agreed with me.

Addressing the group, the storeowner said, "Ladies, we're all here to have a good time. Let's change the subject, shall we? What are your plans for Halloween? Anyone invited to any good costume parties? How about the kids? Anyone got an activity planned for the short people in our lives?"

But the ugly mood lingered. The hard looks the women were throwing at Eloise could not be ignored. Not by me, at least.

Growing up in a home with an alcoholic parent, you learn when to duck and cover. This was definitely one of those time when I wanted to get out of the way of passing bullets.

Eloise scooted her chair closer to mine. Although I considered the matter closed, she continued to explain her behavior. "I had to have more surgeries after the original WLS. After I lost a hundred twenty-five pounds, I was at risk of infections with all that loose skin," Eloise said, pushing a photo my way. "You can get ulcerations. When I walked or moved, the skin moved, too. It was not only uncomfortable, but it also got irritated from the rubbing. I couldn't do all the types of exercises that I both wanted and needed to do because all that extra skin got in my way. Every time I hopped up and down, my sagging skin flapped like wings."

I picked up the picture she passed my way, and quickly wished I hadn't. The image startled me. Eloise stood with her bare arms outstretched, allowing the excess skin to droop from her bones like a pair of bleached out bat wings. A second photo that she shoved my way showed her in a bra and panties. At least, I assumed she was wearing panties because her flaccid tummy skin covered that area. The bulging skin that draped over her knees was truly frightening. I couldn't imagine walking with that sort of padding between my legs.

While I've always been pudgy, I'd never seen photos like those. After reeling from the ugly visuals, a second reaction hit me. I'd never stopped to realize how morbidly obese people must struggle through their daily lives, waging war against their own bodies in attempts to do what most of us accomplish without a second thought.

As that new reality set in, I imagined having all that extra skin removed. Mentally I traced a cutting line along the bottom of

Eloise's arms, across her gut, and between her thighs. How painful would that have been?

*Anguish.* That could only describe it.

"Come on, Eloise." Mel snickered. "You wanted to look better than all of us, didn't you? You like being the center of attention. Cindy's as much to blame as you are. She couldn't stand the idea of having wedding photos taken with a fat mother at her side. And you didn't like having three fat friends."

"I was going to die." Eloise nearly hissed.

"Let me show you the new paper we got in for Halloween." Dodie's voice went up a notch. She was doing her best to steer the Titanic, but the ship was not following her orders. Nope. Instead we were pointing toward an iceberg.

"You were vain!" Karen nearly shouted.

"My diabetes was out of control. My joints hurt so badly that I was in danger of becoming addicted to pain pills," Eloise said.

"See this cute purple and green paper? Aren't these tiny white skeletons on black paper adorable?" Dodie acted as if she couldn't hear the banter between Eloise and her three friends.

"I lost twenty pounds on Weight Watchers," Maggie said, tossing her hat into the ring.

Everyone turned to stare at her.

I bit my tongue. Maggie is a know-it-all. Any problem you have, Maggie can solve. Once she latched onto a subject, she was like a terrier that'd bitten the hem of your pants. She'd never, ever let go.

Don't get me wrong. I like Maggie a lot, but there are times when a little bit of Maggie goes a long way, and a lot of Maggie goes way too far.

"I tried Weight Watchers!" Eloise nearly shrieked. "It didn't work for me!"

"Time for a break!" Dodie shouted. "Everybody get up! Time to stretch! Remember the rule. The treats stay at the food table."

Maggie grinned at me. "Dodie worries that we'll dump food or drinks on our projects. With the exception of those candies in the middle of the table, everything we eat has to be consumed away from our work area."

I followed my pal and the other three women to where Dodie had put out plates, utensils, plastic cups, and a cooler filled with bottles of water and cola. There were also several plastic wrapped plates. The three friends chattered like starlings as they dragged a cooler on wheels out from under the crafting table and over to the food table.

Eloise reached into her purse and put three oranges on the table where she was sitting. They rested there next to her crafting supplies.

"Dodie? May I have a bottle of water? Would you hand one to me?" Eloise got up from her seat and walked closer to Dodie.

"Glad to. Let me dig around in here. I think all the water bottles are on bottom."

Meanwhile, Mel went back to her seat and dug through her handbag. That left her two friends to unwrap the treats they'd baked. Once Mel found what she wanted in her purse, she got up and walked around the table. As she did, she knocked Eloise's oranges onto the floor.

"Your oranges rolled on the floor," Mel said, holding it up for all to see. "I'll wash them off when I take my insulin shot, Eloise."

"Thanks," said the other woman.

The exchange counted as their only civil conversation all evening. Brief though it was, I could see that once upon a time the women had been close friends.

Dodie held up two cold bottles of water. Eloise took one, thanked our hostess, and twisted it open.

"Anyone else?" Dodie waved the remaining bottle.

I was grateful to have it, and I said so.

Karen unpeeled the cover from an aluminum pan. "I brought my homemade banana bread with walnuts and chocolate chips."

Maggie had made low-fat brownies. She urged me to try one. I pronounced it fabulous. "I used pureed prunes and applesauce to cut back on the sugar and fat."

I helped myself to a second brownie while Dodie opened a bag of potato chips and poured them into a bowl.

Angie pulled the plastic wrap off of a container of cupcakes with chocolate icing. Using a spatula, she fixed the frosting on each little treat where it had gone astray. She added candy corn pieces to the icing, one after another. The final product was adorable.

Eloise had an insulated bag under the table next to her feet. She unzipped the bag and got out two smallish plastic containers, one of low-fat dip and another of cut carrots, red bell pepper strips, short stalks of celery, small florets of broccoli, and cauliflower chunks. These she carefully arranged on a rectangular ceramic plate. She peeled the cellophane tape off the dip and opened the lid. When she was done placing every-thing just so, she stuck a tiny plastic flag that said, "Low-fat dip" in the center of the creamy concoction. A silver spoon was set off to one side.

Mel put Eloise's freshly washed oranges back down on the table before joining her friends at the cooler. Once there, Mel strug-gled to get the plastic top off of a large plastic platter. After a bit of tugging and pressing various spots, she finally wrestled the top free. In the center were three conjoined bowls. One contained a creamy con queso dip. Another had guacamole, and the third was full of fresh salsa. Instead of one big serving spoon, she grabbed three plastic ones and stuck one in each dip. Around the outside rim, she added an assortment of baked pita chips and potato chips.

"I'm so sorry. I didn't bring anything," I told Dodie. Even though I'd recently had dinner, I'm always hungry. For me, eating isn't just about food. It's a source of comfort.

"Does it look to you like we don't have enough to share? Or like any of us are going hungry?" Dodie was teasing me when there came a rapping at the front door. A pizza delivery guy stood in the cone-shaped glow of the security light. In one hand was a thickly quilted thermal square emblazoned with the Domino's Pizza logo. However, the stack was too tall to be just a pizza. After Dodie paid the delivery guy, I learned there were two pizzas and a half bucket of wings.

I ate and ate until I needed to unbutton the waistband of my pants. I wasn't alone. Everyone at the table went back for seconds and thirds.

Except for Eloise. She nibbled at a half of a piece of pizza and a handful of veggies with a scant spoonful of dip. After her plate was clean, she peeled one of her oranges carefully and set each delicate section on her dish. Slowly, she ate the pieces one by one. After finishing one orange, she went on to the next until she'd eaten all three. That might seem like a lot, but they were small.

Dodie stayed on her feet the entire time, walking around the table and offering everyone more food.

Mel spoke to our hostess in a low tone. "I put my insulin syringe in an empty plastic water bottle and threw the whole shooting match into your trash can in the bathroom."

Dodie thanked her. "Five minutes, ladies, and then let's get back to work."

It occurred to me that maybe I'd never be any good at scrapbooking, but if this was the way everyone always ate at a crop, I could still come and have fun.

# 4

"What is this?" I pointed to one of Maggie's tools, a flat plastic plate marked with a grid. The tool also had an armature, and an orange slider.

"That's a Fiskars Personal Paper Trimmer. You own one, don't you?"

I shook my head. "No. Can't say that I do. What do you do with it?"

"Anything and everything. I'm not sure I could live without mine." Maggie took a piece of paper, positioned it under the plastic arm, tugged the slider, and to my amazement, the paper was cut perfectly. "You try it."

Maggie has a degree in elementary education. Her voice held a tone of encouragement that probably worked really well with children, but to me seemed condescending. I felt nervous, but gee, what could I do? Refuse her offer?

No way.

I took the implement from her and gave it a whirl.

At first, I fumbled around. There's a lock on the arm that keeps it from flipping up willy-nilly. Maggie showed me how to unlock the mechanism. She pointed to where the cutting line would fall on the paper. Turning the slider upside down, her fingernail edged up to the blade. "This is where all the action starts."

Once I was more familiar with the parts, I cut my first piece of paper. My slice was wobbly.

"Here's a tip." Maggie took the paper trimmer from me. "Keep a steady pressure on the orange slider. Push it to the left or right as you slide it. Choose a side and stay consistent throughout the cut. That way the slider can't wobble in the track. Now try it again."

I wasn't exactly sure what she meant. As I touched the orange slider, she folded her fingers over mine. "See how it wobbles slightly from left to right? Concentrate on keeping it pushed as far right as possible as you move it down the paper. Think 'push right' instead of straight down."

I did, and she was correct. This cut was much neater. From there, Maggie taught me how to mat a photo. She taught me that it's easiest to use photo splits when you are just starting. They come on a roll of waxy paper. Without the right technique, you're more likely to have them stick to you than to your photo. Maggie showed me how to carefully peel off one half of the blue waxed paper backing. I pressed the gummy side of the photo split where I wanted it to go. Once that gummy half was securely stuck to the paper, I peeled off the rest of the waxy blue backing.

For practice, Maggie let me mat a few of her family photos. I quickly realized that if the photo wasn't centered on the mat, by using only one photo split on the mat to tack the picture down, I could peel up the photo and move it around until the edges of the mat were equal on all four sides. Soon, I was zipping along, adding mats to the back of many of her pictures.

Dodie brought over a cellophane package. "Here you go, Sunshine. These are the components for a two-page layout. Knock yourself out. Let's see how you do."

Inside were buttons, pieces of paper, ribbon, and a few stickers. I stared at the mix. It wasn't very appealing to me. The images were too childish. However, I remembered something I was carrying around in my purse. Near the bottom of my bag, I found part of a postcard from a local florist. I'd been carrying around the card around since Easter. The mailer included a picture of an adorable vintage bunny. Borrowing Maggie's smallest pair of scissors, I cut out the creature.

"That's what we call 'fussy cutting,'" Maggie explained. "You can see why."

Yes, I could. I tied ribbon around the rabbit's neck and glued it down.

The printed paper in the cellophane kit was far too loud for my taste. Rather than set the rabbit on top of it, I sliced the gaudy paper into thin strips. These I used as a border for my solid color pages. That kept the bunny front and center. Dipping back into my purse, I found a couple of cotton tip swabs inside my tiny traveling first aid kit. With a twist, I pulled the cotton off of one. This I glued to the bunny to make a fluffy tail.

Instead of using the stickers from the cellophane package on my page, I lined up buttons on a thin strip of green paper. I tucked one end of the green paper under the bunny to ground him so he wasn't floating in space. The rest of the buttons I carefully glued in a row on the facing page. In short order, I was finished. When I glanced up at the wall clock, I was surprised how quickly the minutes had flown. I'd lost all track of time while I was creating.

I leaned back in my chair so Maggie could look over my work.

For the longest time, she said nothing. Not a peep. Finally, Maggie motioned to Dodie. "Come see this."

Dodie stood over me and frowned. The other croppers quit talking. Very carefully, Dodie picked up the two pages I'd created. My heart was in my mouth. Had I done something wrong? Was Dodie going to make fun of me? Why had Maggie been so quiet?

Dodie asked me, "How long have you been scrapbooking?"

"Um, how long have I been here? This is it." Blood rushed to my face. I felt light-headed. Had I made a fool of myself? My pages didn't look anything like the work spread in front of the other crafters.

"This is your first time?" Dodie repeated each word for maximum benefit. "Zounds! You're a natural. Ladies, behold the birth of a superstar."

Dodie held up my page and pointed out the innovative ways I'd used my products. Meanwhile, my face got redder and redder. The more the women complimented me, the more uncomfortable I felt.

"Be right back." Dodie put down my page. As her broad back retreated, I got up and walked over to the bulletin board where she displayed the work of other crafters. Under the cork display panel was a small table with a machine. I later learned it was a die cut machine. Beside the table was a trash can filled with small scraps in a delightful assortment of colors and patterns. My fingers itched to play with them. To the right of the trash can was a recycling bin. Inside were five or six plastic water bottles.

Dodie returned, holding two cellophane wrapped packages under her arm. Brusquely, she shoved the kits into my hands. "Take these. See what you can do with them." One kit had coordinating papers, ribbon, silk flowers, and an entire alphabet of stickers in shades of pink. The other had a vivid purple paper, a green-and-purple patterned paper, a white sheet, a piece of brown string, and a handful of pumpkins cut out of construction paper. I pulled everything out of the cellophane and spread it in front of me.

Maggie glanced over. "Those are the leftovers from previous crops. Dodie always makes a few extra kits. If we mess up or if our kit is missing a piece, we cannibalize the extra kits. You're welcome to use anything from my stash, too. What you have there are pretty slim pickings."

The pink would make a cute page for Anya. The purple might work for Halloween.

Around ten o'clock, I'd finished two more pages while leaving blank spaces for where photos would go. All I had left was one full sheet of patterned pink paper. I was out of ribbon and die cuts. Although Maggie had given me permission to draw from her stash, I didn't want to take her supplies. I knew she was on a tight budget.

A stretch break was in order. I stood up, walked around, and glanced at the sample pages on the walls. Most of the layouts were okay. A few were really cute. Some people tended to slap down stickers willy-nilly all over their pages. One woman had punched star-shaped holes in her photos. She'd actually cut a chunk out of her husband's head, which I took as a sign that she was working out some sort of aggression. She had my total sympathy. I couldn't help but wonder what George was doing tonight. Whatever it was, I suspected that his business partner,

Bill Ballard, was involved, too. Even though I tried not to, I hated that man. There was something about Bill that creeped me out. Each time I saw him, I wanted to take a long, hot shower when I got home. Yuck.

Making a slow circuit of the store, I took a lot of time, examining the layouts and trying to figure out what made some of them outstanding and others more pedestrian. Unfortunately, there weren't a lot of page designs that qualified (in my mind) as good work. Fewer yet were actually creative. Most of the scrapbookers seemed to use the same supplies, over and over again in the same way. I wasn't particularly impressed by the end result.

After my slow turn, I decided to take a potty break. I'd already seen other women head for the back room, so I took off in that direction. I used the toilet and washed my hands. In the trash bin was the empty water bottle with three syringes safely encased inside. I tossed my wet paper towels on top of the mess.

When I got back to the table, Maggie suggested that I buy a pad of scrapbook paper. "That's the best bargain for your money. It's cheaper than buying paper one sheet at a time. Often there are embellishments in the pad. Sometimes there are even alphabets or words. You really get a lot to play with for your dollar."

After looking through the pads of paper and choosing one, I spent the next hour happily creating scrapbook pages. The layouts weren't very exciting, but I did get a chance to practice my new cutting and photo matting skills. Dodie nudged my arm with a fourth cellophane package of paper and supplies. "Here. Take this."

"How much do I owe you?" I'd already paid her for the pad of paper. Even though George assures me that we have plenty of money, I grew up dirt poor, and I don't throw cash around like confetti.

"Not one thing. This is a slightly damaged kit." She gave me a lopsided grin. "Matter of fact, I want to see what you do with this stuff. Have at it."

She'd given me two-sided patterned paper plus coordinating solids, a variety of stickers, ribbon, and buttons. I stared at the selection Dodie'd handed me for what seemed like a long time.

All night I'd been watching women toss away pieces of paper. Most of them were about the size of an index card. Surely those could be put to good use!

"Dodie? Do you mind if I dig through the trash can?" I pointed in the direction I meant.

"Help yourself."

I got up and pawed through the bits and scraps. There was a whole lot of good paper in that trash. More than I'd expected. I was ready to take my haul back to the work table when I took a second look at the recycling bin and decided I simply had to do something with the plastic water bottles.

It took two trips, as I carried my loot to the worktable. Maggie was busy using a heat gun, a sort of super-duper hair dryer, on a stamped image that had been coated with plastic powder. The heat caused the powder to puff up, leaving behind an embossed image. Pretty cool stuff. Since then I've learned that if you spend any time at all around crafts, heat is your friend. You can do all sorts of things, things you haven't imagined, if you can apply a little heat. For example, you can dry emboss, which means you heat powdered plastic so that it puffs up. You can also use an increased temperature to shrink plastics. In fact, most plastic packaging has been either shrunk or stretched into shape. In other words, if I could control the heat, I could manipulate certain plastics and turn them into something new. Of course, I'd need to be careful.

I used a pair of old scissors to cut the bottom off the water bottles from the recycling bin. As I did, I took care to shape the plastic into flower petals. Next, I manipulated a pencil so that I could press down on a molded plastic water bottle bottom. Then I applied an intense stream of hot air. The plastic "petals" shrank appreciatively. Some wanted to curl up, but I alternately used the pencil and the long blades of scissors to hold them flat. When the plastic cooled, I was left with six flattish plastic flowers. These I backed with scrap paper from the trash can. The finished product looked like large, colorful 3-D flowers that I could adhere to my pages. For an additional pop of color, I glued a button to the center of each flower. The ribbon in my pack was bright green, so it became the stems and leaves of my new plastic flowers.

I was totally focused on my task. The entire world disappeared as I worked. I didn't even hear Dodie come up behind me. In fact, I jumped sky-high when she put a hand on my shoulder. "As I live and breathe, Sunshine, you are a prodigy. A real, live scrapbook genius. What an amazing, unique, and thrifty way to decorate a page."

I figured that Dodie was buttering me up so that eventually I would buy a lot of stuff I'd never use. Nevertheless, a warm glow inside me must have lit up my face. I did my best not to break into a huge grin. I couldn't remember the last time someone had praised me without qualification.

After bragging about my work, Dodie signaled it was time for another stretch break. I got up and shook out my hands. Eloise came over to see my pages. "My word. Dodie's right. You are something else."

I could have sworn that Eloise was drunk. Her words were slurred, and her breath stank like booze. After I thanked her, she wandered off toward the bathroom. There was a definite wobble to her gait.

## 5

---

$\mathcal{F}$inally, Dodie told us it was time to stop for the evening. I'd really enjoyed myself, and I couldn't wait to do more. I wondered when she was holding the next scrapbook crop.

Dodie grinned at me as Maggie and I headed for the front door. "I'll expect to see you Wednesday night. I've never seen anyone who took to scrapbooking the way you did."

Mel, Karen, and Angie had packed up quickly and left in one car. Eloise slowly picked up her stuff, putting every item in a designated spot. As Maggie and I walked out into the parking lot, my friend talked me into going back to Jazzercise.

"We miss you. One of the instructors was asking about you the other day."

"I keep intending to go back to class."

"You should. You really should."

I agreed to meet with Maggie on Monday at five-thirty. The Ivy Chapel location for Jazzercise was ideal, as it was halfway between both of our homes. The time was perfect, too, as it happened after our kids were home from school.

Maggie and I lingered at our cars while saying our goodbyes when Eloise came out of the store. She walked past us. Close enough to almost bump into me. Oddly she didn't speak. It was like she didn't notice we were there. In the soft umbrella of light cast by the security lamp, Maggie raised an eyebrow at me and asked, "What gives? She's usually very chatty."

"I don't know her well enough to hazard a guess."

A hollow clatter caused both of us to spin around quickly. Eloise had dropped the ceramic platter that had once held her veggies.

I was closest to Eloise, and I rushed to her side. "Are you okay? Did you cut yourself?"

Maggie trotted to join me. "Eloise? You all right?"

"Sure." But the word was slurred and fuzzy.

"Stay away from the pieces. I'll go get a whisk broom." Maggie morphed into her Superwoman personality. I'd seen this side of her before. When she got this way, it was best to stand back (at least six feet), shut up, and let her do her thing.

I offered Eloise a hand to help her with her belongings but she swatted it away. "I said I'm fine," she snarled. "Is there a problem with your hearing?"

That stunned me. Eloise had gone from sad and friendless to nasty-tempered and mean in less than fifteen minutes. What was her problem? "I was just trying to help."

"If I need help, I'll ask for it." Turning her back to me, she keyed the lock of her metallic blue Kia. As I watched, Eloise fumbled

49

around with her things, while trying to get one hand free to yank open her driver's side door.

"Let me," I said as I stepped up to help.

She moved aside, but as I grabbed the handle, I heard her muttering curse words under her breath. To say I was astonished is to put it mildly. A few of her comments about me were so egregious and coarse that I instinctively backed away. She could drag her own sorry self into her car. Whether her junk followed along or not wasn't my problem.

I wasn't interested in an evening of abuse from a person I scarcely knew. Truth be told, I'd gone to college and left behind my own family unit in an attempt to avoid nasty scenes like this one. Especially once I'd caught a whiff of alcohol on Eloise's breath. Had she lingered with Dodie and shared a drink?

I wondered.

Maggie came out of the store and popped a squat to sweep up the broken ceramic pieces scattered in a wild arc. She held up something silver and waved it around. "Eloise? I think I found one of your spoons."

Eloise shouted, "Leave me alone, Maggie!"

Maggie must have smelled the booze, too, because she tried to position herself between Eloise and her car. "What is your problem, Eloise? I'm not sure you should be driving. Kiki? Go and get Dodie."

I turned on my heel and headed toward the store.

"Maggie, move it," Eloise said. "Back off."

I could hear a scuffle behind me as I stood on the stoop and banged on the back door of the store. No one answered. Dodie was still inside, but for whatever reason, she wasn't responding. Behind me, Eloise and Maggie were yelling at each other.

"Leave me alone!" Eloise yelled, but her voice was muffled behind the closed car door.

Hammering both fists against the back door of the scrapbook store, I tried again to rouse Dodie's attention. This time I succeeded, and she almost knocked me off the stoop when she threw open the door.

"What's up?" Dodie greeted me with a puzzled expression on her face.

Eloise hit her gas pedal hard and rocketing past Maggie. Thank goodness Maggie was nimble enough to jump back out of the way or Eloise would have clipped her!

The wandering beam of Dodie's flashlight caught the dramatic scene. "Whoa. What on earth? Maggie? You okay?"

I jumped off the low step and ran to my friend's side. To my relief, she was unharmed.

"Maggie, do I need to call 911?" Dodie asked.

I could see Maggie trembling. It took her a minute to get her wits about her.

"Maggie?" Dodie asked again.

After a moment, Maggie responded to Dodie. "No. No 911. Eloise was acting so strange. She could have hit me!"

I nodded. "We noticed."

Dodie stepped down the stoop and came over to see for herself that Maggie was all right.

"Eloise walked right past Kiki and me like we weren't there. Then she dropped her serving platter and broke it. You saw me grab the whisk broom. I tried to sweep up the pieces, and when I discovered she'd also dropped a spoon, she got all huffy."

"Huffy? Incensed is more like it," I added. "And there's something else. When Eloise walked past me earlier, I could have sworn she had alcohol on her breath."

"I did, too!" Maggie chimed in.

"That's impossible." Dodie sounded irritated with me as if I'd manufactured a problem. "Look, Sunshine. Your imagination is getting the best of you. There's no way she was drunk. Where did she get something to drink? Unless she pulled a bottle out of her purse, my place is dry. There wasn't any booze at the crop. You know that."

I spread my hands wide in a conciliatory gesture. "I understand what you are saying. But I grew up around drunks, Dodie. She definitely was acting like she'd tied one on, and she smelled like she'd had a drink, too"

Dodie gave a snort of derision. "We were all here. Nobody drank anything but water and cola at my crop. Nobody. I served the drinks myself for that very reason. Eloise might have been tired or upset, but she wasn't drunk."

"It took her a long time to gather her things and get in her car." I wasn't disagreeing with Dodie; I was simply stating a fact.

"That's true," Dodie agreed. "Usually she's fast off the mark. But tonight, she might not have been feeling well. Her friends were pretty rough with her.

"But she smelled like she'd been drinking," Maggie said.

"Maggie's right. Eloise had been really nice most of the evening, but her personality changed from sweet-natured to nasty at some point. Didn't you notice it?" I held up my fingers and ticked off my points. "One, her personality changed. Two, she was wobbling as she walked. Three, she dropped something. Four, she smelled of booze."

"Dodie, shouldn't you call the police?" Maggie asked.

"And say what? That two of my customers are claiming that a third customer was acting like a drunk? And on what basis? I did not personally see Eloise drink any booze. Did either of you see her take a drink?"

The answer to that was no, of course, not. Maggie and I both shook our heads.

"Do you think the cops will do what? Go stop her and give her a breathalyzer test on your say-so?" Dodie's voice grew more and more strident. "Even if I asked them to follow her around, what good would that do? Except to totally tick her off?"

She had a point.

As an expert on avoiding conflict, I had to agree with Dodie. Any action she initiated would surely tick Eloise off. It would not do any good, and it might make a bad situation worse.

Dodie turned off her flashlight. We stood there, letting our eyes adjust to the dark. "Here's the long and short of it. I know Eloise didn't drink any booze. Not on my watch. I'm positive she wasn't served any. Not by me. Not by anyone else. I guess there's always the off chance that she had a bottle in her purse, but short of searching everyone's purse upon arrival, I couldn't possibly know about that. Certainly, I didn't see her drink and neither did the two of you."

"Uh-huh," I said.

Maggie had that mulish look on her face. The one I'd seen only a few times before, but I'd come to fear. I like Maggie a lot, but she can be downright annoying when she wants to.

Dodie saw Maggie's pout, too. She nudged me with an elbow. "Kiki? You didn't see Eloise drinking anything, did you?"

"Nope." I dragged a toe along a crack in the asphalt. "Nothing but that bottle of water. You grabbed that bottle randomly from the ice chest. She took one, and I took the other. But it wasn't like I was watching Eloise's every move. This is all new to me. I was already feeling overwhelmed without paying attention to anyone else."

I cautiously glanced over at my friend. Maggie is a stickler for rules, but even she couldn't see a good reason for us to bug the cops. The dejected slump of her shoulders told me she'd given in.

I CAME HOME to an empty house. The place was totally dark. Given the quiet, sleep should have come easily but I was too keyed up. Between my excitement about scrapbooking and my worries about Eloise, I could not possibly close my eyes. I couldn't even sit still!

Better to use the quiet time productively.

First, I did my prep work for Lily. After spending the evening working with color and patterns, I was definitely in the right mood. Looking over the paint sample strips I'd collected, I put a star next to the colors that appealed to me. I tore pages out of the new magazines. All these went into the folder for Lily.

With a sigh of satisfaction, I could now do exactly what I wanted with the rest of my evening—and that meant I could dig in and scrapbook.

I spread my new scrapbook supplies, meager as they were, on the extra card table in our great room. I opened the magazines I'd purchased, again, but this time, I parsed the images differently. I paid attention to the positioning of the photos, versus the use of the embellishments. I noted the ways people had used pattern and solids.

The leftover supplies from the cellophane kits that Dodie had given me were quickly spread across the card table. There were the pink coordinating papers, ribbon, silk flowers, and an entire alphabet of stickers. Next to those I placed the vivid purple paper, a green-and-purple patterned paper, a white sheet, a piece of brown string, and a handful of pumpkins cut out of construction paper. Only on closer inspection, it wasn't construction paper. It was hefty scrapbook paper.

I moved the pieces around, arranging and rearranging them. Then I did some creative thinking. What went together? What suggested themes to me? What did I need? What could I use that I had here at the house?

I hopped up and went over to the cabinet where I keep a stash of candy. From there, I grabbed two Werthers' Caramel pieces, unwrapping and chewing them slowly. I planned to toss the wrappers, but I noticed that the foil inside the cellophane was gold. I peeled the cellophane away so that all I had left was the foil. Could I use that to make something? Anything? A crown! Wasn't Anya her daddy's little princess? Indeed, she was.

When I went to the trash to toss the cellophane, and that's when I noticed George had tossed in the brown wrapper from his cup of Starbucks coffee. Picking the corrugated paper up, I examined it more carefully. The hills and valleys intrigued me. If you held that wrapper a certain way, the ridges could look like broom bristles. With a plan in mind, I set to work.

Although I hadn't gotten home until after midnight, I stayed up for another two hours, playing with my scrapbooking supplies. For once I was actually happy that Anya was still at her grand-mother's house. Often, I'm a little depressed when I'm alone in the house, but this time I was happily distracted. As I played, I listened for the sound of George's key in the lock, but my husband didn't come home that night. That is to say, he wasn't home when I dragged myself to bed at two-thirty. I know because he would have walked past me on his way to the master bedroom.

Not surprisingly, I slept late the next morning. In fact, I might not have gotten up before noon except that my phone rang. Thinking George might be calling, or that Anya was ready to come home, I answered.

"Kiki? Can you believe it? Isn't it awful?"

The fog of sleep made it tough for me to identify the voice. "What?"

"The news about Eloise," said Maggie. "You've heard, right? And to think she drove off while we were watching."

"W-w-w-what happened?"

"You didn't hear?"

"No. I just woke up. What happened?" I repeated myself.

"I can't believe it. We should have stopped her. I wonder if Dodie will be liable."

Now I was fully awake and totally frustrated. "Maggie, what on earth are you talking about? I don't know what you are trying to tell me! What happened to Eloise?"

"She drove her car into an abutment and died on impact. It must have happened right after she left us there in the store parking lot. The news reporter said they are waiting for toxicology reports. An eyewitness saw her swerving and weaving her way down the highway."

"That's horrible!" I was now fully awake.

"I'm worried that if Eloise was drunk, then Dodie might be legally responsible. I might be, too. Maybe even you."

I rolled my eyes. Trust Maggie to wake me up with the worst possible news ever. I had to nip this in the bud.

"We didn't see her drink anything! She said she was fine."

"We both know she wasn't fine. We saw her drop that plate."

"Right. Haven't you ever dropped anything when you were sober?"

"No." Her voice sounded belligerent.

I felt sick. My stomach churned and knotted. "But we didn't see Eloise drink anything. None of us had any liquor. It's not like we were out at a bar, throwing back beers, and watched her get soused. There was nothing we could have done!"

The more I said, the more upset I became. "I don't have a breath-alyzer in my car, do you? How would we know she'd been drink-ing? We didn't know. We couldn't know. There were no facts to support us."

Even as I tried to defend our actions, I felt like a total jerk.

"Why didn't we stop her?" Maggie's question came out like a sob.

I sniffled back tears. "We didn't stop her because we couldn't. You tried, remember? She out-maneuvered you. We weren't fast enough. She was determined, and let's face it, she was a big woman. She towered over both of us. How could we have stopped her? What if we had knocked her to the ground? Then we would have been liable for hurting her. We were in a no-win situation."

"But she's dead!" Maggie screeched. "Surely we could have done something!"

"What? You tell me, Maggie. What?"

She was silent for a long, long time before volunteering a new perspective. "As soon as I heard the news, I phoned my brother-in-law. He's a lawyer. I explained that I tried to stop her. We didn't see her drink, and we didn't serve her alcohol. We didn't know for sure that she was impaired, and we still don't know the nature of her impairment. It's possible she had a stroke or some bad reaction to medication, and that's what we saw."

"What was his take on this?"

"That any judge would use the actions of a reasonable person as a test. Would a reasonable person have acted the way we did?"

"I think so. Short of tackling her or standing in front of her car, we did everything humanly possible to stop her."

I could imagine Maggie nodding on the other end of the phone. "That's right. We tried. You went back to get Dodie. I fought with her for her keys. She nearly ran over me. We did our best."

"Dead," I repeated. "She's actually dead? Have the cops actually said that Eloise was drunk?"

"The newscaster said the authorities were waiting on toxicology reports. I guess that means they don't know, or they haven't decided if she was drunk or not."

"Oh, wow," I said. "I wonder if Dodie knows what has happened? Maybe we should call the authorities. There's no way the cops would know that Eloise was coming from a crop."

"That makes sense. Tell you what. I'm going to call Dodie. You still planning to come to Jazzercise on Monday?"

"Sure. Why not? Maybe we'll know more by then."

Maggie's sigh was heartfelt. "I hope so."

# 6

eorge didn't show up until noon the next day, which was Sunday. He was wearing the same clothes as he'd worn when he left the house on Friday.

I'd been sitting at the kitchen counter making a list of furniture pieces I thought the house needed when he tried to slip past me. However, I'm not blind and I'm not deaf. I'd heard the garage door close, the door to the house open, and the soft *pat-pat-pat* of his shoes on our floor. I waited until George was nearly even with me before yelling, "Hey?"

He froze.

"Hel-lo," I sang out. "If you were trying to sneak past me, you have failed miserably, George."

Slowly, he turned to face me, except he didn't look me in the eyes.

"Long, long business meeting, huh?"

"Um..." Crimson crept up his throat. He studied the floor.

"This is ridiculous, George. You're acting like a tom cat. Maybe I should have expected as much. You and I weren't exactly a love match."

"Kiki, I…" But he didn't continue. What could he say?

"Okay, let's be honest with each other. I know I'm not your soul mate. I'm not your ideal woman." My voice shook a little, but I kept talking, "Your mother doesn't much like me."

"Actually she's — "

"Save it, George. I just want what's best for Anya. Could you please come home before she wakes up? Granted, she's with your mother right now. I suppose this one is a gimme, but in the future, let's keep our marriage in the same category as Disney movies and fairytales and happy ever after, okay?"

That's when I broke down crying. On top of the news about Eloise, this was really too much for me to handle. It's one thing to pretend your marriage is fine, and another whole thing to finally admit you're living one big lie.

George babbled nonsense about not wanting to wake me up, car trouble, thorny business problems, zoning issues, global warming, ebola outbreaks, and international currency fluctuations. I wiped my eyes as I sat stoically through his baloney. Sprinkled in between were copious apologies. I hit the mental "yada-yada-yada" button when he got to those.

Using the hem of my tee shirt, I blotted my eyes. When he reached over to rub my shoulder, I shrugged him away. All morning long, I'd wondered when he'd show up and what he'd say. I'd even entertained fantasies that he was hurt or lying in a gutter somewhere. After all, Eloise hadn't made it home. Maybe

George had met a similar fate. His sudden appearance had been an anti-climax.

I wasn't sure what he expected me to say or do. Did he think he could talk me out of being upset? Maybe he thought he could convince me I was wrong and he'd been working all night.

I didn't care. I'd had a bellyful of his bad behavior. I got up, poured myself a glass of cold water, gulped it down, and walked out of the kitchen.

George followed me. He didn't skip a beat. On and on he went about mitigating factors. I made it to the top of the stairs and then I lost it.

"Just shut up, George. You're only making matters worse."

I'd never spoken to him like that. Somehow it felt oddly satisfying.

Not surprisingly, we avoided each other the rest of the day. Our conversation was limited to polite requests, like, "Would you turn up the thermostat?" Nothing more.

By the time Sheila brought Anya home Sunday night after dinner, a definite chill had settled in the air. Not surprisingly, George was more than happy to make two trips to his mother's car. He carried in loads of shopping bags. Anya picked up on the tension between me and her father right away. She waited until her grandmother was in the bathroom to ask what the problem was.

"Did you two have a fight?" Those denim blue eyes of hers bore into mine.

"No." George was quick to respond. Coming up behind her. "A difference of opinion. That's all."

Our daughter cocked her head like a robin watching a worm. I could almost see the wheels turning in her brain as she tried to decide whether a difference of opinion qualified as a fight or not.

Meanwhile, Sheila had walked out of the bathroom, past me and into our kitchen. Of course, she hadn't bothered with a greeting on her way into our home. Why would she? I was part of the drywall as far as she was concerned. Her decision to move the discussion to our kitchen table felt like a silent command, and we all trailed behind her like ducklings on parade.

Suddenly my shoulders drooped and exhaustion flooded me. Keeping up the pretense that we were a happy family took a lot of energy. Tears threatened from behind my eyes, and I would have let them flood, but Anya was watching me intently. So instead of crying, I pinched my nose as hard as I could. I would carry on, acting like nothing was wrong, because she deserved a happy childhood.

To get my mind off the subject of her father's late night prowling, I asked Anya, "Tell me about the shopping you did. Did you find something to wear to homecoming?" I did my best to sound chipper.

"We did." Sheila often answered for my daughter. This time she sounded bored. "I found the cutest royal blue plaid skirt for her. Anya looks absolutely adorable in it. With the white blouse I got her and the golden-yellow cardigan we found at Macy's, she'll fit right in. There are golden-yellow suede loafers in one of the shopping bags as well. I'm thinking she should wear her tiny pearl charm on a gold chain as an accessory."

Trust Sheila to dress our child from head to toe.

"Mom? I got my ears pierced." Anya pulled back her hair to show us two swollen ear lobes.

My gag reflex nearly got the best of me. In my book, ear piercing was an action reserved for when you turned sixteen. If Sheila had asked, I would have told her that I wanted Anya to wait.

But she didn't ask.

Instead, my mother-in-law had acted as though she was the person in charge, and I was the bystander. Slow anger built up inside me. Would it have been too much trouble for Sheila to phone me and ask what I thought? Wouldn't that have been the respectful way to handle this? Or had she bypassed parental input all together? Had Sheila called George and gotten permission from him? Maybe George had withheld the conversation. Did it even cross his mind and his mother's mind that I should have a say in my daughter's piercings?

Anya looked at me expectantly, waiting for me to comment on her ears. The bright light in her eyes told me she was thrilled with this new sign of her impending adulthood.

"I see. That's, um, exciting. I assume you got a special cleanser to use to help them heal." I admired the twin pearls my daughter wore. At least Sheila had chosen tasteful earrings as a starter pair.

"Yes. The lady at Claire's showed me how to keep my ears from getting infected. Gran bought me five pairs of earrings from Macy's. Real gold."

"Uh-huh." I decided not to say anything to Sheila while Anya was preening over her new jewelry. Instead, I'd talk to George later. A glance over at his green-hued skin told me that he was feeling pretty sick at his stomach. Bodily functions usually have that effect on him. The flaking crust of blood at the tip of Anya's earlobe was enough to make my husband toss his cookies.

"How nice," I used my voice to convey that the conversation was over.

"I'm going upstairs to unpack my new stuff." Anya gave us a weak smile as she rose from her chair.

"Do your ears hurt?" I asked.

"They are sore." Her smile flickered.

"Let's get you a Tylenol."

I didn't say any more than that. As I walked out of the kitchen, I glanced over my shoulder. George was shifting his weight nervously, squirming in his chair.

Would he confront his mother about her overstepping her boundaries?

I doubted it.

Sheila left shortly afterwards. Remembering my manners, I thanked her once again for going shopping with Anya. Even though my words were polite, my emotions were strained, and Sheila knew it.

George did, too.

I was so steamed about Sheila's overstepping her boundaries that I avoided talking to George for the rest of the evening. Fighting in front of Anya was not on my agenda, and anything I had to say was bound to come out wrong. Since my husband and I hadn't really spoken all weekend, I didn't tell him about my scrapbooking misadventure. He had no idea that I'd watch-an impaired woman climb in her car and drive away before killing herself.

Instead, he had pussy-footed around me, being extraordinarily polite and solicitous. He could tell I was on the verge of losing my self-control, so he gave me a wide berth. He assumed I was going to complain about Sheila. I certainly had a good reason to be angry with her. But Sheila's bad behavior had been the icing on my cake. The real problem, the real worry grinding me down, was the death of Eloise Silverman. My problems with Sheila were simply part of the ongoing fabric of my life.

Rather than deal with my disrespectful family, I put on a smile that was as phony as it was tiresome and went about my life as if nothing happened.

~

MONDAY MORNING DAWNED frosty inside our house. George got up first, started coffee, and met me as I came down the stairs.

"Look, I know you're sore about Mom taking Anya to Claire's without asking our permission."

I made the universal "cut" sign by dragging a finger across my throat. "Save it." Taking a detour around him, I headed for the coffee, following the fabulous smell of roasted beans.

"But Kiki, I'm trying to apologize."

"But George, you didn't create the problem. Your mother did. You apologize for something she did."

elf out, buddy. Not that it matters. Point being, as no respect for me. None at all. She treats me like I am a baby-carrying surrogate who stuck around too long after she got her paycheck."

"That's not fair."

"True. It's not fair. Actually, it's totally unfair...to me. My husband stays out all night, and his mother walks all over me. But hey, things are looking up. Lily Grey is going to show up later today and make my life hunky-dory! Picture perfect on the outside!"

That sailed right over his head. "Are you ready for her visit? I can reschedule."

"Inconvenience the divine Miss Grey? Not on your life. I'm ready and rearing to go. See?" I reached into the cabinet under the sink and pulled out a file folder. "I've done my homework. I made a list of furniture that I think we need. I tore out photos from magazines to show her styles I like. I even stopped by Home Depot and chose paint swatches. Not that I expect Lily to pay any attention to me. Nobody else does. Why should she feel any obligation?"

I slapped the decorating folder down onto the counter.

George came up behind me. I could feel his presence. Gently, he put both hands on my shoulders. "Please. I don't want you to feel like this. You have every right to be upset. I'll talk to Mom. We both can do better. You deserve our respect. Anya is growing into a wonderful young lady, and that's on you. I'm sorry that Mom and I don't show you the respect you're due."

He'd never said that before. All the anger drained from me, leaving me like an empty vessel. Tears swelled in my eyes and spilled down my face. The lump in my throat made it hard to swallow.

"I'm sorry, too." I wiped away the tears.

George squeezed my shoulders. "You have no reason to apologize. My mother did this. It's on her."

"Mom? Dad?" Anya called from the bottom of the stairs.

George and I jumped apart the way two guilty lovers do. Simultaneously, we turned toward our child. She's usually a slow waker-upper, but this morning she fairly bounced into the kitchen. "I couldn't wait to wear this new outfit that Gran got me."

Anya twirled around, showing off a faux leather skirt and striped turtleneck. She looked cute as all get out. Sheila had done a magnificent job of dressing my child. I remember being a preteen. We hadn't had any money, so I'd sewn all my clothes and done a poor job of it. By contrast, Anya could have stepped off the pages of any fashion magazine.

"You look marvelous, darling," I said in a phony accent.

"Your mom's right. You look terrific." George hugged our daughter. "Is all that new?"

"Every bit of it."

"I hope you thanked your grandmother."

"I did."

George volunteered to drive Anya to school. That was fine by me. I kissed our daughter goodbye and did as I always do. I st--- d of laundry. A lot of people hate folding, but I find Today I took extra time to stroke flat the towels, warmth transfer into my hands. I wished I had ge about Eloise. Of all the sad aspects of our hurt the most was the realization that I didn't have a partner in my life. Not really. I kept a lot from him, partially because I felt he didn't truly care about me. This was one of those times when I desperately needed someone to talk with. I felt horrible about Eloise's death. I worried that I might have some legal liability for not stopping her. Even if I didn't have a legal liability, it sure seemed that I'd had a moral one. And I'd failed the woman. Okay, it wasn't like I knew her well, but she was another human being, and I'd let her down.

Hadn't I?

Despite all of his flaws, George was a good and decent man. I ached to share my burden. I wanted to hear what he thought and hoped he would help me absolve myself of the burden of responsibility.

I DID AS many laundry loads as I could and raced around picking up the house in preparation for Lily Grey's visit. George pulled into the garage seconds before Lily rang the doorbell. I'll give her this, she arrived promptly at eleven. George answered the door. I walked into the foyer in time to see Lily throw her arms around my husband's neck and plant a big kiss on his cheek, barely missing his mouth. To make matters worse, she hung onto his arm, sinking her polished talons into his suit jacket.

"Hello, Lily." I stepped up and offered her my hand, effectively putting a wedge between her and George.

The designer stepped away from George and gave me an up-and-down once over. However, she did not offer to return my handshake. "Kitty, right?"

"Kiki." George spoke clearly and authoritatively. "You know her name. In fact, you have my wife's name in your file."

Lily pursed her lips and pouted prettily. "Right. Okay. Where would you and Kelly like to sit, George?"

"Kiki," he repeated with a whole lot less patience and more emphasis.

"Sorry." She shook her head like a wet collie does, flicking off any semblance of concern about my name. "George, honey? What had you decided? I brought notes from last time we talked."

*Last time they talked?* Did she mean that she and George had spoken? Or had Sheila had been involved?

Lily continued, "Your mother had so many terrific ideas that I almost ran out of paper. Do you have some place where we can talk?"

Yes, I thought, I have a place you can talk. It's one of the seven circles of hell. Take George with you when you go, okay?

All this discussion about furnishing our home had happened behind my back. My face was turning red with anger. For a half a heartbeat, I considered turning on my heel and storming out of the room. Just as quickly, I realized that stomping off now would mean I'd capitulated. Sheila and Lily would have won. I'd be out of their way. They could do as they wished, and I'd be stuck living with the results of their mutual admiration society.

Instead of walking away from the situation, I stood my ground. Lily regarded me coolly, but George spread his hands in a placating type of way. "Lily? I realize my mother has a lot of ideas about what she wants, but this is *our* home, Kiki's and mine. I know my wife has done copious prep work, so I suggest we go into the kitchen and sit down. Then we can discuss what Kiki would like."

"But I've already gone over all this with Sheila." Lily didn't speak; she whined.

"I told you at the start of this project that Kiki would be involved. This is her home, after all."

"Right." Lily dug the toe of her pump into the floor and twisted it the way a little girl does when she's wheedling to get her way. "Naturally, I figured that you meant Kimmy would get to approve everything once I selected it."

"No." George's tone took on a severity I'd never heard before. "*Involved* means Kiki has input at every stage of the job. If you'll recall, I specifically explained that while I welcome my mother's ideas, this is not her house. It's ours." With that he slid an arm around my shoulders. The weight of it felt good. I lifted my chin a bit higher and met Lily's gaze without flinching.

Lily muttered under her breath. Batting her lashes at George, she tried again. "Oh, George. I've put so many, many hours of work into this project already. Wait until you see all the fabulous selections—"

"Great!" George said with enthusiasm. "Kiki and I will be happy to look them over."

Lily pouted.

George jerked his head toward our kitchen. "Come on. Let's go and sit down at the table. I want you to see what Kiki has picked out to give you guidance, Lily."

As George and I headed toward the kitchen, I could have sworn I saw Lily stick out her tongue.

---

## 7

*A*lthough I wouldn't call Lily a good listener, she'd been cowed enough by George that she pretended to care what I said. That was a start. Each time she interrupted me, I raised my voice and said, "Excuse me, but I wasn't done speaking." Sticking her lower lip out in a pout, she could shut up and let me talk.

At the end of a tense hour, Lily'd taken a few notes and tucked my file inside of hers. As the three of us walked toward the front door, Lily played with her hair, flipping it and stroking it in a totally unprofessional way. Between that and batting her eyes at George, the woman must have burned two hundred calories, easy.

Before she left, Lily told George that she'd have prices and images for him to review a week later. George cleared his throat and let out a deep and exasperated sigh. "For Kiki to review. Of course, I'll be there, too."

"For Kendra to review." Lily was nothing if not consistent when it came to ignoring my name in favor of any other label she could dream up.

"Kiki." George corrected her. "Please give my wife your business card, Lily. Just in case."

Right. Over the next seven days I might have a hankering to decorate a mausoleum, and if that happened, guess who I'd call?

When the front door was firmly locked behind Lily, George shook his head. A gurgle of laughter bubbled up. "I knew she could be a pain in the butt, but honestly, I've never seen Lily act like that."

I shrugged. I should have said, "Thanks for standing up for me," but I didn't. After all, he and his mother had met with Lily without me. His recent good behavior came under the heading of, "Clean up in Aisle 6."

George left for work, and our honking big house suddenly seemed very empty, so I decided to do my grocery shopping for the week.

By nature, I'm an introvert. I don't need a lot of people in my life. I enjoy spending time alone. I love to read, to color, and do small craft projects.

As I waited in the checkout line, I perused the magazines. Peering inside them was always the highpoint of my shopping trips. I'm probably the only person in the grocery store who chooses the longest line at the cashier's station on purpose because it gives me time to flip through the periodicals. Those colorful covers always promise that the contents will definitely change my life.

Today my eyes skipped from low fat meals to cats to retirement living to sewing to gardening and finally landed on scrapbooking.

Impulsively, I picked up the new magazine on scrapbooking and tossed it into my cart. As I did, I smiled to myself because already this new hobby was starting to take over my life.

Slowly the checkout line moved forward. The customer in front of me put a plastic divider on the belt. Without looking at the clerk, I unloaded my groceries.

After my cart was empty, I took the time to greet the checker. Her name badge said, "TawNee." The girl was large, easily over two hundred pounds. She mumbled, "Hi, how are you? Did you find everything you need?" As she ran the goods over the scanner, she never looked at me. Not once.

It occurred to me how being overweight makes you invisible. In our culture, weighing too much is simply unacceptable. Although I felt empathetic, the cashier expected me to be judgmental. Not once did she engage with me, person to person, and I knew why. With excess weight, there comes a deep and abiding shame. When you aren't thin, you spend every waking moment beating yourself up. You call yourself names. You imagine that other people are putting you down, too.

I also noticed this was the only checkout lane without a bagger. Rather than stand there twiddling my thumbs, I picked up my purchases and bagged them myself. As I touched each item, I did a tiny mental calculation: Was this healthy or should I feel embarrassed? When I grabbed the half gallon of butter pecan ice cream, I blurted out, "This is for my husband. It's his favorite."

George rarely eats ice cream. I, on the other hand, eat a pint at one go.

TawNee slowly raised her eyes to mine. "Uh-huh."

For a half a heartbeat, we studied each other. Two overweight women in a world where thin is in. Both of us felt the weight of shame pressing down on us. Rather than greeting each other as two people, we'd reduced ourselves to failures, the product of a society where it's almost impossible to lose weight.

A tiny voice inside me cried, "I'm better than this!"

I hated myself for the fat-shaming response that was a part of how I interacted with others. Right then and there, I decided to do something different. Something bold.

"How's your day going, TawNee?"

There. I'd said it. I'd called her by name and treated her like a human being.

She froze while ripping the paper receipt off her register. "My day?"

Emboldened I said, "Yes. Your day. How's it going? I'm going to try something new. I'm going to my second scrapbook class Wednesday evening. Have you ever been to one?"

The corners of her lips twitched. Her eyes brightened. Before my very eyes, TawNee came to life. "Once."

"Was it fun?"

She thought a sec. "Yeah. Yeah, it was."

"Good. I'm a little intimidated. I'll be stepping out of my comfort zone."

TawNee broke into a big grin. "Don't be. You'll have a blast."

~

AT HOME, I quickly unloaded the groceries. The magazine
beckoned; I sat it aside. After getting all the cold items refriger-
ated, I shelved the rest.

Putting a nice placemat on our counter, I served myself the big
pre-made salad I'd purchased. Although I ached to open the
scrapbooking magazine, I'd promised myself to eat slowly and
enjoy my food. The scrapbook magazine would be my dessert.

I'd been honest with TawNee. Attending my second crop would
mean taking yet another step out of my comfort zone. Perhaps
my initial luck with layouts had been beginner's luck. Maybe I'd
exhausted all my talent. If I went back to the scrapbook store, I'd
spend money. George never complained, but still I felt guilty
because I wasn't bringing money in. Wasn't that a good enough
reason to stay home?

I held the phone in my hand and considered calling Dodie and
canceling my reservation for the Wednesday night crop. If
necessary, I could use Eloise's accident as my reason for not
going. I could say I'd found her death too disturbing.

That would be a lie. It would also be unkind to Dodie. It wasn't
her fault that Eloise had died.

I reviewed my original reasons for attending my first scrapbook
class. The primary one was that I needed to be a good role
model. My daughter needed to see me making friends and
having hobbies and interests. For too long, I'd excelled at rolling
over and playing dead. What was that famous saying by

Clementine Paddleford? *Never grow a wishbone, daughter, where your backbone ought to be?*

Clementine made a good point. I'd been acting like a limp noodle.

I lectured my inner introvert. "You can do this, and you need to do it. Anya needs a strong mother as a role model. She needs to see you having women friends, finding hobbies and interests, and spending time with other adults. After all these years at home, it's time to plan for an adventure. Or two. Or three."

The salad was good, although bland. Munching through cup after cup of lettuce makes me feel like a cow that's grazing in a field. Boring! Since I'd put the magazine aside for later, I turned on the flat screen TV.

At the top of the news was a report about Eloise Silverman's fatal auto crash. She'd slammed into the rebar bracing an overpass only two miles from Dodie's store. According to the perky blonde who was talking into the microphone, "Mrs. Silverman was under the influence of narcotics and alcohol at the time of the car crash."

That was impossible! There must have been a mistake. Where did she get the drugs and the booze?

When the camera panned to the mangled car, my breath caught in my throat. The forensics specialist who spoke with the reporter confirmed that Eloise hadn't slowed down before hitting the abutment. In fact, his tests proved she'd actually speeded up.

"Was this a case of intentional self-harm?" The blonde frowned as much as she could with a face full of Botox.

"That remains to be seen. Investigators will take their time completing a forensic psychological review of Mrs. Silverman's state of mind. As we speak, they're conducting interviews. Assessments like this take time."

The reporter signed off, and the news continued with a weather report.

Was it possible that Eloise had planned her accident all along? She had sounded wistful when talking about her daughter moving away. Her husband had left her, too. Perhaps the cruelest blow of all had been how all her friends turned on her. Possibly that had been the final straw.

Whatever happened, however it happened, the experts had determined that Eloise had ingested drugs and alcohol before she climbed into her car.

The lingering question was, how?

ONCE I FINISHED my chores around the house, I rewarded myself by looking over my new magazine and re-reading the other scrapbook magazines. The articles explaining archival safety really caught my attention.

Certain properties of paper, such as lignin, caused it to become brittle. This compromised the strength of the fibers, and in return, caused photos to fall apart. The Ph of paper, adhesives, and developing chemicals also were factors that harmed and could eventually destroy images.

In one way, the destruction didn't matter too much when you had copies of photos stored digitally. However, if you were talking about priceless family heirlooms, any loss of clarity was a huge problem.

Adding to the problem of fading images was the natural process of fading memories. Sure, a box full of photos was a grand inheritance, but if nobody could identify the faces in the pictures, their meaning was lost.

For all these reasons, modern scrapbooking had become a popular pastime. When you worked on your photos while getting together with friends, you could enjoy yourself while preserving your family's heritage.

Scrapbookers seemed to fall into two main camps. From what I could tell, purists only wanted to use materials proven to be archivally safe. Fun-seekers weren't so worried about archival safety because they'd decided they had enough copies of photos to waste a few here and there. A third camp was a blend of the two philosophies. These scrapbookers were careful to preserve old, one-of-a-kind family images, but allowed themselves free rein when working with newer pictures.

After reading through the magazines, I set them aside. I decided to work with the materials I had and make a list of what I thought I needed to move forward.

I'd dumped everything onto the card table that functioned as our kitchen table when the doorbell rang.

Sheila stood on our front steps.

"Good afternoon." I moved aside to let her pass.

Instead of greeting me, she cocked her head and studied me as if she'd never seen me before. "I heard you were rude to Lily Grey."

My eyebrows climbed nearly to my hairline. "You heard what?"

"Lily phoned me in tears. She said she's never been so rudely treated in her entire life. I wouldn't be surprised if she refuses to work with George or Dimont again. Ever."

This stunner rocked me on my heels. By no stretch of the imagination could I see Lily as an injured party. In my estimation, *she* had been rude to me. George could back me up on that. I opened my mouth to say as much, but Sheila beat me to the gut punch. "Kiki, you do realize that Lily's father is one of the biggest real estate moguls in the St. Louis area, don't you?"

"Uh..." The answer was a flat out, "No," but I stuttered around with a mushy noncommittal response.

"Eugene Grey owns more land than the Indians did. That's how Lily got her start. She designed houses for her dad."

As Sheila spoke, she encroached on my personal space. I kept backing up, trying to put distance between us. She continued, "If George and Bill want to buy more land to develop, they need to play nicely with Lily. Your little stunt this morning might have cost them both dearly. Honestly. How could you be so stupid? And selfish? And self-serving? That big section of land out by Chesterfield is nearly theirs. But it won't be if Lily runs to her daddy and complains."

Drawing herself up with a sniff and a snarl, Sheila stared down at me. "For goodness sake. Use your head. If George and Bill get the rights to build on that piece of property, you'll be set for life. If not, well, you've condemned everyone to begging for crumbs."

"I didn't..." I couldn't find the words. I meant to say, "I didn't know." A little voice of rebellion piped up and reminded me that nothing I could say would matter. Unless Sheila was flat-out wrong, Lily was going to make me pay for not groveling at her feet.

While Sheila glared at me, I sorted through my options. I could tell her that Lily had been unspeakably rude to me. I could tell her to talk to George. I could tell her that this was a matter between my husband and me.

Yeah, right. Like any of that would matter if George and Bill lost the big deal they'd been working on for months. Whatever Lily said, true or not, didn't matter. If she told her father to stop the deal from going through, my family would suffer. Truth comes in second to power. Lily held all the cards. I was sitting at the table with a nothing-burger hand.

As for suggesting that Sheila phone George and get to the heart of the matter, well, why bother? What possible good could that do? Even if he backed me up, I was smart enough to see that I would lose by winning. The minute that George had asked Lily to decorate our house, my opinions had taken a back seat to her clout.

Sheila fairly hissed at me as she let the stale air out of her lungs. "I think I have soothed her ruffled feathers. I have begged her to overlook you."

Yup. She said, "Overlook you." Not "overlook your poor manners" or "overlook your misguided attempts to be treated like a human being." *Overlook you*, as in me. Treat me like I was a squashed bug on the windshield of life.

"She's promised to think the situation over. I've sent her a dozen yellow roses and signed them with your name. I've assured her that she can work with me, as I'm both reasonable and knowledgeable. Under no circumstances does she need to bother with you."

Talk about kicking someone when she was down. Sheila had landed a mean jab in my ribs.

"Now I'm going to go pick up my granddaughter after school. She's going to have dinner with me. I suggest that you make yourself scarce the next time Lily visits. We don't want to encourage Lily to spread word of your misbehavior around CALA, do we?"

"No." It came out like a whisper, but it was loud enough for Sheila to hear.

Having secured my permission to be ignored, Sheila left, slamming my door behind her.

I ARRIVED a few minutes late to Jazzercise. Thank goodness for the upbeat music and the motivating instructor! Because I hadn't been there in a while, my old "spot" had been taken. Coming in late didn't help; the room was crowded. I wedged myself into a small space in the back of the room where it was hard to see the instructor. Being in the back was disappointing because Ivy Chapel's social hall has a huge window that looks out over a beautiful scene. From my spot, I could only enjoy the tops of the trees.

Even so, I was happy to be in class and dancing to the music. Sheila's visit had shaken me to my core. While one part of me ached to protest, another realized she might very well have a point. I didn't know the dynamics of this city. I'd seen enough to realize families were interrelated and ties ran deep. Of course, I didn't want to ruin George's business. That had been the last thing on my mind.

As I turned over Sheila's accusations, I missed a step and wound up nearly bumping into another exerciser. That was a reminder I needed to push aside all thoughts of Lily Grey. I needed to concentrate. The moves in Jazzercise aren't intricate, but they are complicated enough that you need to pay attention. That's one of the under-appreciated benefits. Following the choreography keeps your brain engaged. For a full hour, I could set my cares aside.

When our class ended, Maggie wandered over to where I was rolling up my mat. "I didn't see you come in."

"I was late," I managed while huffing and puffing.

"Got time to run to Bread Co.?" She pronounced the casual dining chain the way St. Louis natives do, making "co." rhyme with "dough."

"Sure."

Once we'd ordered and taken seats in a nearby booth, Maggie's mood changed. The positive endorphins from exercise started to wane. Real life overcame her. We were both damp from sweat, but now our breathing was less labored. Since we'd danced our hearts out, we could enjoy the freshly baked treats we'd ordered. While s clerk plated our food, both Maggie and I sniffed the air appreciatively, inhaling the tantalizing fragrance of yeast, sugar, and butter.

"I can't believe what they're saying about Eloise, can you?"

"I heard drugs and alcohol."

"A blood alcohol content of .16%." Maggie hunched over the table, moving close to me and keeping her voice low.

"How did she manage to imbibe that much booze? And take any pills? While we were watching? Did she do that in the bathroom?" I kept one eye on the counter, waiting for the server to call out our names as a signal that our food was ready. "I don't recall her using the restroom, unless she did it while we were talking in the parking lot. And if that's the case, would Dodie have noticed?"

"I looked it up, and by my calculations, to get a blood alcohol that high, she would have downed seven beers or so. We know that's not possible." Maggie frowned. "Where'd she get them? How had she guzzled them in front of us?"

"And what did she do with the empties? Did they find them in her car?"

Our orders were ready. The server set a tray on top of the counter and called out, "Maggie? Kiki?"

I hopped up to get our tray, but first I looked the food over to make sure everything was correct. I had asked for a pumpkin muffie and an iced green tea. Maggie had ordered a bran muffin and a water. I thanked the server and carried the tray to our booth.

"Thanks for grabbing that." Maggie pushed napkins my way.

"No problem. Do you think Dodie knows more about what happened than we do? Seems to me that the cops will most certainly want to talk to her."

Maggie nodded vigorously. "My brother-in-law Paul is a cop over in Maryland Heights."

"I thought your brother-in-law was an attorney."

"I have three brothers-in-law. One is a cop, one is an attorney, and the third grows dope. I asked the cop, and he said they might even want to talk to all of us. Everyone who attended the crop. He told me he'll try to find out if there were empty bottles in Eloise's car. As you can guess, the car is pretty smashed up. I suppose it's possible she drank just a little bit of booze, but mixed it with medication she'd taken earlier. Or she could have had booze in her car all along. She could have left the crop, pulled off the highway, drank the booze, and got back on the road before hitting the abutment."

"Does the timing work? Would that have given her enough time to get to the spot where the wreck happened?"

Maggie lifted one shoulder and let it drop. "I don't know. When you consider how much she must have consumed, seems like she would have been sitting at the side of the road for a while. A long while. I know it would take me hours to drink that much."

"That's because you're not drinking to get drunk. If your goal was expressly to get inebriated, you wouldn't take your time, would you? In fact, if you planned to kill yourself, maybe you'd want to drink as fast as possible so you couldn't change your mind." I hated pointing that out, but it needed to be considered.

Maggie fingered a raisin that had fallen out of her muffin. "That raises another problem. I didn't know Eloise well, but she didn't seem like a psychopath. Not to me at least."

"Huh?"

"She had to realize she might hurt somebody, right? Eloise didn't strike me as a person who didn't care about causing other people pain. Quite the opposite."

I thought that hurting other people meant you were a sociopath, but correcting Maggie was an impossible task. Instead, I focused on what she meant. "So you're suggesting that if you wanted to kill yourself by getting into a car accident, you'd do it someplace more remote? Less busy?"

"Exactly." Maggie nibbled on the raisin. Her dark eyes had grown even darker as she thought about the consequences of Eloise's accident. "She could have wiped out an entire family. I just didn't get the impression she was reckless that way. Did you?"

I thought about what little I knew of Eloise. "You're right. She struck me as someone who was sensitive. Easily hurt. Folks like that are usually empathetic."

"Then is it remotely possible she wasn't trying to commit suicide? That she didn't drink all that booze on purpose? Could it be that someone slipped her a mickey?" Maggie's whole face tightened with intensity. "Do you catch my drift?"

"Whoa." I rocked back in my seat, causing the vinyl booth to squeak. "You're wondering whether Eloise Silverman was murdered?"

## 8

---

*I* didn't get to talk to George that evening. He called to say he was working late. Sheila phoned to ask if Anya could stay overnight.

Without my husband and my child, the house felt barn-like in size, which it was, and emptier than usual. Fortunately, George had gotten me a Kindle for Hanukkah, and I'd loaded it up with books. The idea of being able to carry an entire library in my handbag had appealed to me. The reality was even better than I had hoped. I'm a fast reader, so my Kindle was like having a virtual pile of books at my fingertips. Pure heaven. I made myself a peanut butter, Nutella, and banana sandwich. Life didn't get much better than a book and a fabulous meal.

I fell asleep on the futon, waking up to a nightmare about Lily Grey decorating our house like a barnyard. Fortunately, George walked through the door about then. He shook me gently. With tears in my eyes, I told him about the dream.

"Your mother dropped by. She explained that Lily's dad is really important. Without his blessing, you'll lose out on a big deal."

ing room, all I could see was his silhouette.

eys and took a long time answering me.

ed the situation. This deal will be good for

ey as well as for us. Lily played the drama queen card

en she talked to Mom. I didn't hear about their conversation until a few hours ago. I would have asked Mom to keep out of it, but..."

His voice trailed off. "Mom's been a big help to us, getting the business started and all. Drawing a line and keeping her on her own side has been impossible."

He added, "Seems like all I do is apologize to you. Look, I don't want you to live in a house you hate. You pass your ideas on to me. I promise to show you what Lily proposes. I don't mind being the man in the middle. If that's what it takes to make this work, fine."

"Peacemaker, huh?"

He laughed. "I guess. Keeping Lily happy isn't my highest priority, but Mom does have a good point. If I get on the wrong side of Lily, that's unhelpful. Is that a word? Unhelpful?"

"Beats me."

I scooted over, and he sat next to me on the futon. I told him about Eloise Silverman. In the dark, talking came naturally. I wanted to share the suspicions that Maggie and I had conjured up. George listened carefully. "Keep out of it, Kiki. If there is a murderer involved, you don't want to be his next victim. Or her next victim. Although I can't for the life of me see why anyone would want to hurt Mrs. Silverman. I've known her for decades. Not very well, of course, but she did attend our temple."

"I might not have a choice. Maggie thinks the cops will want to interview all of us."

"Probably. The person most at risk here is Dodie Goldfader. What was she thinking letting a drunk customer get in a car and drive off?"

"That's the point, George. We had no reason to suspect she was drunk. Eloise drank her bottle of water in front of us. She only ate oranges that she brought from home."

"Hmm. This is a real head-scratcher." He patted me on the knee. "I'm done for the day. Going to bed. Are you coming?" He held out his hand to me.

That was an invitation.

I took him up on it.

Because Anya had spent the night at her grandmother's house, I didn't see my daughter until I picked her up after school on Tuesday. My kid bubbled over with excitement about the upcoming bonfire, a tradition at CALA.

"Mom, you won't believe all the stuff they're doing for home-coming. Planting mums along the driveway. Decorating the halls. We've been practicing the school song for weeks now. Our English teacher is having a contest. We have to memorize a poem and recite it in front of everybody. The person who does the best will get up in chapel and present the poem in front of a big audience. Alums and teachers and parents and students. Best of all, there's a middle school sock hop on Friday night. Can I go? Please?"

"Let me check with your father."

That was an excuse designed to buy me time. The idea of my child mingling with boys in a dark gymnasium made my palms sweat. However, I didn't want to be the Mean Mom. I also wanted to go to the Friday night scrapbooking crop. Letting Anya attend the sock hop would be good for both of us. She'd be at a school activity and I'd be working on my new hobby. George and Sheila both had repeatedly stressed the importance of Anya fitting in at CALA. Rather than bring the subject up with George, I waited until after supper and phoned Maggie. I asked her how well-chaperoned the sock hops were.

"You don't need to worry. I'm chaperoning. It means I'll miss the Friday night crop, but it can't be helped. I'll be at the crop tomorrow night. How about you?"

"Yes," I said impulsively.

"You know, Anya is welcome to come spend the night with Mathilda after the dance. That way you won't have to hang around outside the school, waiting for the dance to end. At least one of us can go to the scrapbook store for the Friday night crop."

"That's a very kind offer. I think we'll take you up on it." I knew George wouldn't object, especially after I told him that Maggie and her hubby would be in attendance. "Have you heard any more about Eloise?"

Maggie whispered into the phone. "Just a little. My brother-in-law the cop says the authorities are definitely leaning toward foul play."

"What? Why?"

"The forensic psychologist evaluated the evidence and concluded Eloise was not suicidal. She'd recently put a deposit on an Alaskan cruise. Did you know she'd signed up to go to a scrapbook conference up in Michigan?"

"Nope."

"The day before the accident, she'd checked a bestseller out from the library. She'd even mentioned to the woman working at the front desk that she hoped to read the book and get it back to the library in a week, because she knew other people were in line to read it. Who does that if she's planning on driving her car into a wall of concrete? Oh, and one other thing. She'd recently had her car serviced and put new tires on. See? Those are all indicators that she expected her life to continue. Eloise was definitely making plans for the future."

"What about her state of mind immediately after the crop?" I wondered if the cruel comments from her former friends had unbalanced the woman's emotional equilibrium.

"The police have asked to talk to her three friends. Angie already gave them a voluntary statement. She explained that Karen and Eloise often butted heads, but in general all four of the women got along well. In fact, they wanted Eloise to start riding to crops with them again. She said not until they apologized to her. Angie swore up and down that Eloise was fine when she left the store."

"But we know better. We saw how messed up she was."

"Karen used to be a registered nurse. She told the cops that Eloise had an inner ear problem that caused her to have occasional problems with her balance. Other than that, she confirmed that Eloise was fine. Although she did say that Eloise might have had a stash of liquor in her car. Karen said it's natural for weight loss candidates to trade one addiction for another. A local doctor who's an expert backed her up. He says it's amazing how many people go from problems with food to substance abuse. As you've probably guessed, overeating is only one part of the problem. At the root is a secondary problem that causes women and men to try to numb themselves. Either they eat or they drink or they take drugs. Or a combination of all three."

Maggie delivered this gush of information in a perfectly flat tone. Clearly, she'd accepted what she'd learned from her brother-in-law. As sure as she sounded, I wasn't convinced.

"But Maggie, did they find empty booze bottles in her car? And how can that account for her being tipsy immediately after she left the crop? At the end of the evening? We both thought she'd been drinking. But when did she get drunk? It couldn't have been at the crop. She couldn't have ducked out to her car and grabbed a bottle, chugged it, and returned. We were with her the whole time. It doesn't make sense."

"Let's go over the facts. You smelled booze on her breath near the end of the crop. She was definitely not herself in the parking lot. That means she must have ingested the alcohol while she was at the store." After a "huh" of exasperation, Maggie added, "Look, just because we didn't see her drink alcohol doesn't mean it didn't happen, right?"

I had to admit that was true. After planning to sit by each other at the Wednesday night crop, we said our goodbyes and hung up. I told myself, "Some things don't have answers. That's why they call them mysteries. Get over it, Kiki."

Try as I might, I couldn't help but feel sorry for Dodie. It sounded like the authorities had made their decision that Eloise was not suicidal. That being the case, they were stuck working their way through another scenario. If Eloise didn't kill herself, there was only one conclusion: Someone else had murdered Eloise Silverman. Someone who'd been there with us at the crop that night.

Lucky, lucky me. I'd found myself a new hobby. One I shared with a stone-cold killer.

TUESDAY EVENING FLEW BY. George made it home in time for dinner, a quick meal of sandwiches and chips. After Anya went to bed, I listened to the news, but I didn't hear anything else about Eloise or her death.

George disappeared into his office. He was still working when I went upstairs to the spare bedroom. The next morning, he'd already left for work before I rolled out of bed. I told Anya about the Earharts' invitation while I was driving her to school. Her face fell a little.

"Mathilda's not my favorite person. I'd rather spend the night with Nicci Moore."

"I realize that, sweetheart."

"Mattie Earhart thinks she knows it all."

I bit my lip rather than say, "She comes by that naturally." Instead, I asked, "Do you want to stay home? Or go to the sock hop and let me pick you up?"

Anya sighed, a sound so deep and sad that I shot her a quick look. "Nah. It's nice of Mrs. Earhart to invite me. It's better than sitting home, I guess. I really wish that Nicci Moore was my best friend."

"Have you asked her to do things with you?"

A side-wise look from my daughter curdled my stomach. "Of course, I have. She thinks I'm stupid."

"I doubt that," I said to myself. I did the best I could to bolster my daughter's spirits before she climbed out of the car and trudged the sidewalk that led to her school. As I pulled away from the curb, I realized that someone would need to watch Anya this evening if I was going to make it to the crop at Time in a Bottle. After I parked my car in our garage, I sent George a message and asked him to pick up our daughter after school.

He wisely shot a message right back, saying that he was happy to give me the night off.

Back at the house, I puttered around with the supplies that Dodie had given me and the paltry items I'd purchased. In the end, I put all my supplies in an old tote bag I'd had for years. It wasn't as sporty as the wheeled bags the other women used, but it would do for now. Since I had a lot of time before the crop, I decided to do the rest of the laundry. In between loads, I went online and looked at decorating schemes that might work for our house.

I didn't get a phone call canceling the Wednesday night crop, so I compartmentalized everything related to Eloise Silverman's death.

I took a seat at the crafting table and saved one for Maggie. I'd no more than settled in when Mel, Angie, and Karen arrived. None of them looked like they had been crying. That seemed odd to me. Why weren't they upset about Eloise? I was, and I barely knew the woman.

Maggie and I might not have burst into tears, but both of us were upset about Eloise's death. Why weren't her friends equally torn up?

If that was how good friends acted when you were dead, maybe I was better off without any female pals. Given their callous behavior, I decided to have a re-think about trying to meet new people.

Maggie came racing in. "Getting out of the house gets harder every day," she said.

A woman named Vanessa Johnson took a seat at the end of the table, next to Maggie. We were ready to start when the front door flew open, and another woman ran in and grabbed the empty chair next to mine. Dodie introduced the newcomer as Bonnie Gossage.

I was the only person who didn't arrive with tons of toys, so I felt a little naked and amateurish compared to the others. Bonnie seemed to realize what was happening, because she leaned close to me and whispered, "Glad to have you. Don't worry about not having enough toys. You'll catch up."

Dodie welcomed us. "As some of you know, we lost a friend recently. I'll miss Eloise Silverman. I'm sure I'm not alone. If you'd like to sign a card for her family, I have one at the front counter."

Bonnie, Vanessa, Maggie, and I immediately walked to the front counter. None of Eloise's friends moved. Not a one. You would never have guessed they'd once been best buds. *Color me shocked.*

Dodie showed us a technique called masking. It sounded complicated, but it really wasn't. A mask is a way of covering up something, either a portion of an existing image or an area on paper. It's a useful rubber stamping technique. Rubber stamps are a thrifty way to stretch your scrapbooking dollar because you can use them over and over. They're versatile because you can change the color of ink so that the finished images match your layout.

As Dodie passed around a basket of stamps, I remembered that Anya had gotten a set from Sheila her birthday. I wondered if any of them could be useful when scrapbooking. That got me really excited. Maybe I actually had more scrapbooking supplies than I realized!

Dodie gave us several sheets of plain white copier paper to practice on. I jotted down the steps I used:

1. I chose a stamp with a paisley pattern and another stamp of a peacock. I wanted my finished peacock to have a paisley tail.
2. I stamped the peacock on a piece of copier paper. I cut out the entire image of the peacock, and then I cut around his tail very carefully, so it came off in one piece. (This gave me a peacock's head, body, and legs as one piece AND a tail that was a separate piece. Both of these two pieces of copier paper could be used as "masks.") I put the peacock's body to one side.
3. I put repositionable glue on the mask of my peacock's tail and stuck the tail portion ONLY to a piece of good scrapbook paper, where I wanted my finished peacock to go. Once the tail mask was on the paper, I could use the tail shape to block out or "mask" anything I stamped on top of it.

4. I inked the entire peacock stamp once more, lined it up with the "mask" of the tail on the nice paper, and stamped over the tail.

5. After giving the ink a second to dry, I peeled away the "mask" of the tail. That left me with a nicely stamped peacock head, body, and legs but minus the tail.

6. I added repositionable adhesive to the original peacock's body (the head, body and legs without a tail) that I'd cut from copier paper. I carefully put that nearly whole peacock (but without a tail) on TOP of the new peacock I'd just stamped on good paper.

7. Then I inked the paisley pattern and stamped it on top of the cut-out peacock without a tail. This way, the paisley pattern filled in the area of the tail.

TA-DA! I now had a peacock with a paisley tail. I'd been totally focused on what I was doing, so didn't stop to see what the other students were trying to accomplish. Dodie was walking among them. She realized I was done and asked me to hold up my paper.

There were gasps of appreciation. "Sunshine, would you mind walking around and showing other people how this works? There's only one of me."

I did. I went clockwise around the table because Dodie was working counterclockwise, starting with Maggie, who was struggling with the technique. I went over to help Angie, who was staring off into space. From the disarray of materials in front of her, I guessed she hadn't paid much attention to Dodie's demonstration. Maybe at least one of Eloise's friends truly cared about her.

"Hi, are you interested in seeing what I did?"

"Sure." Her words and her facial expression didn't match.

Rather than question her about what she'd retained, I showed Angie the peacock I'd stamped with his paisley tail. "Here are the masks I used. See how they worked together? Is there a special combination of stamps you'd like to try?"

I dragged over the basket of stamps so Angie could look at them and choose a couple. I guess she hadn't gotten the memo, because Angie looked into the basket but didn't make a selection.

"Angie? Do any of these images appeal to you?"

Realizing that I wasn't going away, she dangled her hand in the box and pulled out an hourglass. "This sort of does. It's an hourglass, right? I wonder what it would be like to turn back time. To have a second chance."

Looking up at me, she seemed to issue a challenge. "Can you fill this with sand?"

"I can try." Oops. I corrected myself. "We can try, that is."

I dug through the basket. Eventually I turned up a landscape dotted with sandpipers frolicking on a sandy beach.

"I bet we can get this to work. We can use the beach from this stamp to create the sand that runs through the hourglass."

Patiently, I explained the masking process to Angie. Her eyes filled with tears. I knew she was thinking about Eloise. I grabbed a box of tissues from the table behind us and handed it to Angie.

"Thanks," she said.

Dodie looked over at us. Her eyes darkened with sympathy. Obviously, she had been in similar situations more than once. That gave me courage, and I decided not to give up. I'd show Angie the process, and keep my fingers crossed that in so doing, I'd distract her from her grief.

Rather than listing the steps again, I broke the process down and walked her through it one step at a time. Even that seemed challenging. Angie could barely ink her stamp. When she pressed the inked surface to the scrap paper, all she got was a blob.

"I think you've over-inked the raised image." Grabbing a paper towel, I cleaned off a lot of the ink. "How about trying again?"

The second time, I practically took her hand in mine. With my help, Angie was able to position her stamp in the right place.

Holding up the finished image, she displayed it for her friends. "Cool, huh? Think about it. Just last Friday, Eloise was sitting here with us, talking about her WLS."

"Can you imagine spending that much money on yourself?" Mel gave a bitter laugh.

"I don't know." Dodie shook her head. "Poor health is expensive, too. Eloise told me she desperately wanted to live long enough to see her daughter get married. Her doctor told her she wouldn't make it that long unless she did something dramatic."

"What a crock!" Karen hooted. "All of us know better. Eloise had that surgery because she wanted to look good. That's the long and short of it. Vain, vain, vain."

"Is that so wrong? Don't we all want to look our best?" Bonnie Gossage looked up from her project and stared at Karen. "When you combine the desire to look better with a doctor's recommendation to lose weight, that's a powerful incentive isn't it? Sure, surgery is expensive, but what's a human life worth?"

Angie's face turned red. She did not like being challenged. "It's one thing to want to get healthy. It's another to spend tons of money because you are determined to steal the limelight from your daughter at her wedding. You should have seen the slinky dress that Eloise wore! She made a spectacle of herself."

"How did she get the money?" I asked. The way these women talked about the money that Eloise spent, I wondered if she'd borrowed it from them!

A silence descended over the group. No one would meet my eyes. After a long wait, Dodie said, "Eloise used her own money, the inheritance that her father left her, and paid for the surgery she needed to save her own life. Is that what all of you heard, too?"

That brought a mumbled agreement from Karen, Angie, and Mel.

"I don't understand. If Eloise's father wanted her to have the money, wasn't the inheritance hers to do with as she pleased?" I asked.

Mel glared at me. "She should have used that money for her family!"

"Why?" I asked. "Her father didn't leave it to her family. He left it to her. Was there some sort of need that went unmet because Eloise decided to have the surgery?"

The uneasy quiet that followed suggested the answer was, "Of course not."

"Ben wanted to buy a boat." Angie nearly spat out. "He begged her to let him buy it. He'd even put a deposit down on a model he liked. Eloise should have let her husband decide how to spend that money! That poor man supported her and their daughter for thirty years! What Eloise did was purely selfish. The whole family could have enjoyed a boat."

That didn't make a bit of sense to me.

And yet it did.

In our society, a "good" woman is expected to put other people first and herself last. Always. Eloise had infuriated her friends by breaking that unwritten rule.

Her women friends were furious.

Or were they jealous?

Was it possible they envied her?

I wasn't sure which one was true.

"I assume you'll want to do a little shopping before we leave the store?" Maggie raised an eyebrow. "Dodie? Don't you have a list of suggested supplies for beginners?"

"Start with this," and Dodie handed me a photocopied sheet of paper and another cellophane package. "Come on. I'll help you find everything."

# DODIE'S LIST OF SUPPLIES

DODIE'S LIST OF SUPPLIES FOR BEGINNING
SCRAPBOOKERS

1. Pads of scrapbook paper — Typically this is the cheapest way to buy paper, especially when compared to buying single sheets. Many pads offer coordinated papers and embellishments as a bonus.
2. Fiskars Personal Paper Trimmer — Incredibly useful for cutting a straight line.
3. Photo splits — The easiest way to attach photos to paper.
4. Plastic page protectors — Best purchased in packages so you get a price break. These protect your photos and your layouts.
5. A Sakura ink pen — These archivally safe pens won't change colors or fade. Perfect for journaling.
6. A simple, lined journaling stamp — The plainer, the better. With one of these and a pen, you can journal on all your pages.
7. Archival black ink pad — For using with the journaling stamp.

"Of course," Dodie said, "this list assumes you have pencils at home, a good eraser, a pair of scissors, and a ruler."

"Of course," I said with a nod. "What about an album?"

"Do you have a three-ring binder?"

"Sure." I remembered seeing an empty one next to the bookcase in George's office.

"Much as it pains me to say, you should start with that instead of an album. A lot of scrapbookers spend a ton on an expensive strap-bound album. Those are difficult to load, and really, you don't need one when you're starting out. A three-ring binder is more versatile. The 8½-by-11 inches size is easier for most people than a 12-by-12 inches page. The square 12-by-12 inches shape lends itself to boring layouts, whereas the size of a traditional piece of paper forces you to choose a focal point."

I stared at the plastic basket I was holding. Dodie had loaded it with supplies. "This is all I need? Really?"

"Really. Sure, I'd love for you to spend more money, but it's to my benefit to have you feeling good about your new hobby rather than overwhelmed."

I could see how that was true.

"Too often, scrapbookers go home with all sorts of supplies they'll never use. They get intimidated by their supplies. That's silly, but it's true. I'd rather you start with a smaller amount of supplies and feel good about what you do with them. To tell you the truth, Sunshine, I really like what you did with your first projects. I'm eager to see what you do with this stuff. I'm always looking for people to add to our design team. See that cellophane package? I stuck it in your basket. Inside are all the elements our design team is using this month. Consider this a tryout. There's no charge for those supplies. Can you take photos? Any good at it?"

"Don't get her started," said Maggie. "Kiki is always taking pictures. She tends to focus on the weirdest things, too. I don't mean to be unkind, but she finds stuff interesting that most of us walk right past."

"Such as?" Dodie handed me the plastic basket and crossed her arms over her chest. She's a very hairy woman, and I was temporarily fascinated by the furry appearance of her skin. I quickly realized Dodie was waiting to hear me explain why Maggie thought my photos were weird.

"I like to get close-ups of interesting architectural details. Take shots from different angles. Capture interesting and odd signs. Mainly, I enjoy taking photos when people aren't posing. Candid pictures say so much about a person."

Dodie nodded enthusiastically. "You'll have to bring your photos with you the next time you visit. You are planning to come back, aren't you?"

I couldn't see any reason I wouldn't want to come back. Dodie had been nice enough. I have always liked doing crafts, and hadn't my daughter suggested that I get a hobby?

Maggie reached over and patted my shoulder. "Of course, she's coming back. Kiki plans to be here Friday night. Why not sign up right now? Otherwise, you could arrive and find the table full. You got lucky this visit."

"Pass the sign-up pad, Maggie," said Dodie to Maggie, who was sitting at the other end of the table.

Just like that I became a scrapbooker.

# 9
_____

$\mathcal{M}$aggie was still making her choices after the crop, so I wandered around the store, too. Everyone else had left but Dodie, and she assured us we could take our time. My friend studied the photocopied sheet of supplies that Dodie had suggested.

"That's really a pretty good list. Dodie has refined it several times."

Maggie was particularly impressed with how Dodie had specified starting with 8½-by-11 inches finished scrapbook pages. "She's so smart."

"Why?"

"Lots of reasons. Since it's not a symmetrical size, your pages are less likely to look boring. "When you have a 12-by-12 inches page, or an 8-by-8 inches page, it's easy to make the layout too symmetrical, and often that can look boring."

Maggie picked up two pieces of 12-by-12-inches paper. One was a solid pink. The other was a pink and aqua pattern. She put the patterned paper into her paper trimmer. "Here's another reason that 11-by-8½ inches size is good for beginners."

She sliced off one inch from the bottom of the 12-inch sheet. Then she rotated the page and sliced off a 2½-inch strip.

Putting all three pieces aside, she did the same with the solid pink sheet, turning it into three pieces.

"Now you have two 8½-by-11 inches background sheets. You also have extra pieces to use for embellishing your page." With that, she showed me how I could glue the 8½-by-2½ inches strip down the side of the 8½-by-11 inches pieces. Even if I didn't do anything more, the pages looked cute. Immediately I could see why Dodie had suggested the 8½-by-11 inches page size. Each time I bought two coordinating papers, I would be able to decorate two full backgrounds without any trouble.

Maggie crossed her arms over her chest. "It's also smart to have you use a regular three-ring binder for your first album. A lot of store owners would be happy to see you dump a ton of money on a fancy album. But expensive albums can be intimidating. A ring-binder will save you a lot of money. When you feel more confident, you can move on and buy a fancy album."

While Maggie finished her shopping, I filled the basket over my arm with two more pads of paper that I liked.

Dodie saw the contents of my basket. "You might want to bring in your photos and match them to paper."

Dodie rang up my purchases. In the distance, a siren wailed.

Dodie paused to listen. "We're so close to Highway 40 that we hear that all the time. Usually, it's no one I know. I can't believe that Eloise is actually dead. I keep thinking she'll walk through the front door."

"It's hard, isn't it? One minute a person is alive and the next, she's gone. You don't realize how delicate life is. Hers was snuffed out like a candle on a birthday cake."

"That's exactly right."

"None of her friends seemed to care. That really surprised me."

Dodie shrugged. "We're all different."

I could tell she was holding back rather than sharing exactly what she thought.

Because I'd signed up for the next week's crop, I wasn't too worried about figuring out how to use my new supplies. Dodie handed me a schedule and invited me to come back during the week. "I always have time to help customers. Even if I'm busy, I can show you how to use a lot of the tools we keep here at the store. Don't be shy! You want to get off to a good start, so you enjoy what you're doing."

Maggie agreed. "Get to know your supplies. For now, practice, practice, practice."

The total came to fifty dollars, the most I can ever remember spending on something frivolous for myself. Who knew that fifty dollars' worth of scrapbooking materials even existed! Even as I signed the receipt, I realized that I'd had a great time picking and choosing supplies.

I justified the haul by reminding myself that I never spend money like that. *Never*. I can't stand to buy myself anything expensive. First of all, I grew up poor, and I understand the value of a dollar. Secondly, I'm too fat. So nice clothes are out of the question. Third, it's George's money, not mine. Even though he says I have a right to it, I still feel weird.

All that aside, I realized that this I could justify because I was doing the scrapbooks for Anya. Not for me.

After I thanked the store owner for her help, Maggie said, "We'll walk you to your car, Dodie. You shouldn't walk out alone when it's dark like this."

I hadn't been keeping track of the time. A glance at the clock on the wall of the shop told me it was nearly ten. Was that even possible? I'd been scrapping since seven and had lost all track of time. The three of us strolled out into the night, keeping a close watch on our surroundings. Dodie climbed into the lone car in a far corner, a beat-up old Toyota. After she got situated, she turned on her headlamps to light up the parking lot. Maggie climbed into her brown Ford Explorer, while I got into my gold Lexus SUV. One by one, we pulled out of the parking lot.

THERE HADN'T BEEN much to eat at this crop, not like there'd been on Friday evening. When I got onto the highway, my stomach growled, so I took an exit and found a Wendy's with a drive-through window.

The burger and fries smelled fantastic as they sat on the passenger's seat. I took little sips from my Diet Dr Pepper to make it last longer. I didn't want to run out of the drink before I made it to the house.

Once I got home, I went down into the basement and grabbed the second card table, one that I'd found at a resale shop. Previously, I'd used it for wrapping holiday presents. This evening, I hauled it up the stairs, bumping and nicking my shins as I climbed each step. George's car was in the garage, but the TV was quiet, so I figured he'd gone to bed early. I'd peeked in on Anya and found her sound asleep as well.

Being as quiet as I could, I set up the card table right next to the kitchen table. A second trip to the basement added a folding metal chair to my new workspace. As I munched a dill pickle that had fallen off the sandwich, I fantasized about having my very own craft room. It could easily be done. We had five bedrooms and a full basement, so allocating one to me shouldn't be problematic. Except that I'd have to find money for a work-table, file cabinets, and a good light. Suddenly, my mouth went dry and a lump formed in my throat. I absolutely hated asking George for anything. Anything! I felt like I'd tricked him into marriage, so how could I be deserving of a good life?

I felt overwhelmed with guilt and disappointment. Still holding the burger, I wiped away tears with the back of my hand. What good was this big house if the people in it weren't happy? What difference did it make to have a well-to-do husband if I felt awful spending any money? Who cared whether I had an adorable daughter if she thought of me as trailer park trash?

The burger soothed my aching heart. I chewed it slowly. But I was missing something. I grabbed a big bottle of catsup, and doused the fries with catsup. I love French fries, especially with catsup and lots of salt. All the while I was eating, I told myself not to be such a sad sack. Instead, I should count my blessings.

After all, over the past week I'd renewed my friendship with Maggie Earhart. I'd gone back to Jazzercise. I'd met new people. I'd gotten out of my comfort zone. I'd tried my hand at a new hobby. I had a good reason to go back to Time in a Bottle.

Dodie Goldfader had been nice to me. However, there'd been this expression in her eyes, a sort of pity, or maybe even speculation. That unnerved me. Maybe she stared at me that way because I had sort of wandered in off the streets. If I wanted to put a positive spin on the whole shebang, perhaps she'd looked at me that way because she was amazed at how well I'd done, even though scrapbooking was a new craft for me.

Yeah, that might be it. Along with finding a new hobby, I really needed to be more positive.

Reaching back into the Wendy's bag, I pulled out a paper napkin. After dabbing my eyes, I went downstairs for the third time that evening. In neatly labeled boxes, I had photos I'd taken of Anya. I carried two of these upstairs and sat them carefully on the card table. Then I went into the nearby powder room and thoroughly washed my hands to remove any grease and tomato gunk. After drying my fingers on a towel, I opened the boxes and looked through the photos. I found a dozen that I really liked and that were in focus.

Whatever else was wrong in my life, I was the mother to a beautiful daughter.

That was more than most people had.

I had a lot for which to be grateful. My supplies were at the top of my list. I continued to organize my photos and the paper I'd purchased.

By then, it was past one, and I felt sleepy. If I made a mistake with my photos, I'd ruin them. No telling where the negatives were. Perhaps it was time to go to bed.

Tomorrow was Thursday. I'd have the whole day to myself. That would then give me one entire day to buy more magazines and look at photos before I went to my next crop.

On that cheerful note, I fell asleep.

~

Rolling off my mattress and onto the floor, I literally hit the ground running. I brushed my teeth, washed my face, dragged a brush through my hair, put on undies, and pulled on an old pair of jeans and a tee.

Anya came downstairs a few minutes later. "Where were you last night?" she asked in an accusatory tone.

"Didn't your dad tell you? I was at the scrapbook store. Want to see the pages I made?"

She's not at her best in the morning, but seeing herself as the star of my scrapbook pages did wonders for her mood. George joined us, and he too, was impressed.

We talked about the memories we had of the photos I'd used. When Anya ran back upstairs to grab her backpack, George gave me a hug. "I'm glad you enjoy what you're doing. I don't know anything about it, but those pages look terrific to me."

"You don't mind that I spent money on supplies?"

"Kiki, I'm happy when you're happy. You are always thrifty. Go ahead and buy what you need."

That put a grin on my face.

After they left, I sank down into one of the folding chairs at the card table. We had an open floor plan with a pony wall between the kitchen and the great room. This arrangement allowed you to watch TV from the kitchen, a design feature I didn't particularly like because if someone was watching TV, the person cooking was watching TV, too. This morning, I turned on the news in the hopes of hearing more about Eloise's accident.

While I was staring at the screen, Sheila called. "I'm going to pick up Anya after school and keep her with me overnight. We still have a lot of shopping to do."

"Good morning, Sheila. How are you?" This was my typical response to her rude behavior. Here's my theory: I can't change another person's behavior, but I can make it blatantly clear that I won't join her by acting like a twit.

"Yes, well, I'm fine." She was always flustered when I spoke so kindly to her.

"Thanks for letting me know, and thanks for taking Anya. I'm sure she will enjoy spending time with you."

"Right. Okay."

That meant I had a nice long day ahead of me. But first, I needed to check, "So you're planning to feed Anya dinner?"

I thought I understood what Sheila was telling me, but I didn't want to make any assumptions.

"Yes, I will. Linnea baked a chicken yesterday. She made a brisket for today and a lot of vegetables. I have salad fixings."

"Good. Thanks for spending time with Anya."

"Why wouldn't I? She's my grandchild." With that, Sheila sniffed —she actually made a tiny snorting sound into the phone—and then she hung up.

I cleared the folding card table that served as our kitchen table, shoved the second card table next to it, and began assembling scrapbook pages.

Around noon, I realized I had run out of paper, and I was having a blast. I had the perfect excuse for another visit to Time in a Bottle.

∾

THE PARKING LOT for Time in a Bottle was full. Every type of vehicle, late and old models, was represented. After circling the block twice, I parked around the corner in the residential area in front of a house.

Inside the store was humming. I found myself elbow-to-elbow with other shoppers. Since I didn't really know what I needed, the crowd pushed me this way and that. Instead of fighting it, I decided to go with the flow. I also watched the other customers carefully, seeing what their favorite products were.

Since I'd gone through an entire pad of coordinated papers, buying more pads was a safe bet. Similar pads with nothing but solids also appealed to me.

By then I realized that once again I needed a shopping basket to carry my finds. None were available, so I stationed myself by the checkout counter and took one as another customer paid for her purchases.

With that plastic basket over my arm, I looked like a serious shopper, and the other customers got out of my way.

I bought glue runners, Elmer's Craft Glue sticks, a corner rounding punch, a craft knife and blades, a second archivally safe ink pen, letter stickers in three sizes, and two technique books. I knew I had ribbon at home. I also had an old silk floral arrangement that we'd been given as a wedding gift. I hated it, but I could easily take the flowers off and add them to my pages.

I considered a jar of buttons. However, George had put three old shirts in a bag for Goodwill. I could easily take the buttons from them. More page protectors were a necessity. I threw in three packages of them.

Despite the recommendations I'd had for using a three-ring binder, I was tempted by several of the nice albums on display. However, the strap-binding system seemed daunting. Another customer watched me fiddle with the straps.

"Those are really hard to use. If you decide you want to change the order of your photos, you have to take the whole shooting match apart. On the other hand, if you're doing a family album and you're sure you have everything in chronological order, they're perfect."

"I'm just getting started."

"Then I suggest you pass on those and go with one of the ring binder or the post styles. You can always get a strap-bound album later."

She picked up a tiny plastic package. "These are the post extenders. They allow you to get more pages in an album. For the money, they're a great buy."

After thanking her, I popped the post extenders and a gray post-bound album in my basket. I knew I would be ready for the big leagues of scrapbooking soon enough to fill it.

"What else do you suggest?"

She looked over my haul. "A pen with white ink. It will come in really handy for writing on dark paper."

My new friend walked me over to a display of pens and showed me one that she particularly liked. She also pointed to Glue

Dots. "These are great for adhering items that don't have flat surfaces, like silk flowers or ribbon."

Since I'd already decided to use both types of embellishments, Glue Dots seemed like a great idea. I thanked the woman for her help and walked over to the checkout counter.

"Hello, Sunshine!" Dodie greeted me with a big smile when I set the basket on the counter. "Looks like you've taken to scrap-booking in a big, big way."

"I guess you could say that. I've already used a lot of the supplies I got last night."

"I can't wait to see what you did with them."

"And I can't wait to show them to you."

Dodie leaned closer. "If you can, come back on a Monday. The store's never busy then. You can try a lot of the tools before you spend money on them. A few aren't worth buying. I stock them because people get used to them and it's not worth arguing about."

"Sounds great."

## 10

---

*I* spent the rest of the day working on scrapbook pages. Since Anya had opted to spend the night with her grandmother, it was perfect for me to dig into scrapbooking in a big way.

First, I organized all my photos. As much as possible, I put them in date order. After that, I pulled photos by category. For example, we went to the St. Louis Zoo at least once a year, so I pulled all the pictures with the zoo in them. These would make a good setting specific album.

After I organized the photos, I paired up patterned papers and solids. These I cut so that I had three final pieces per sheet. That gave me plenty of paper to dress up my pages with colorful borders. One border I braided paper together. On another, I used the thin 1-inch wide strip and added punched out circles over it in a random pattern. I was quite pleased that I used the hole punch we'd had forever to make the little circles. When I finished, I realized that the empty circles on the strip of paper were actually pretty cute. I backed the empty holes with other paper for a cute bit of trim.

Even though I had limited tools, I had a lot of fun trying new ideas. In fact, looking back on it, I'd say that everyone should work with limited tools at the start. The paucity of tools made me crank up my creativity to the max. It was a lot of fun to challenge myself that way.

I worked late Thursday night and got up early Friday morning and started again.

I didn't see George until he wandered downstairs around nine and fixed himself breakfast. I'd taken over both of the card tables, but he didn't care. He pulled up an old bar stool that had seen him through college. With it pushed against the kitchen counter, he could comfortably eat his scrambled eggs, lox, cream cheese and bagel.

Wandering over to where I was working, he stopped and looked. "You do realize, don't you, that I came home last night at seven and you didn't even realize I was here?"

No, I hadn't even noticed him.

SHEILA DROPPED off Anya at four. As I met her on the doorstep, my mother-in-law pushed a paper bag toward me.

Anya said, "Hi, Mom," and raced past me up the stairs.

Sheila didn't come in. She simply stood there in my doorway. "Linnea cooked too much brisket. She sent some of it over to you. It's in the insulated bag."

"God bless, Linnea." I said it and meant it with all sincerity. I loved Sheila's maid. She'd worked for the Lowensteins for nearly two decades, and she'd watched George grow up. A lot of people in Ladue have maids. That's not unusual, I guess. Linnea was more than the hired help. She was a fixture.

Maybe we got along because we were both outsiders. We also had a religious bond. She's black and attends an AME (African Methodist Episcopal) Church and I'm Episcopalian by upbringing. Every once in a while, we'd get a wild hare and decide to sing hymns in Sheila's kitchen. Although my mother-in-law didn't like it, she did not dare to chastise Linnea. After all, Linnea kept Sheila's household running like a finely-tuned luxury car. Quite honestly, Sheila would be lost without her.

Sheila also pushed two large shopping bags and the thermal bag my way. "The shopping bags are clothes for Anya. She'll want to be appropriately dressed for the homecoming festivities and the dance at CALA tonight. You do remember that the school colors are gold and blue, don't you?"

"Yes." I took all of the bags. "Thank you. Did you want to come in? It sounds like your car is still running, but I can turn it off for you if you'd like to step in and see George."

Sheila cocked an eyebrow at me. "No. I did want you to know that I've smoothed things over with Lily Grey. She's agreed to keep working on your house. Lily has excellent taste. As long as you let her do what she recommends, this place will be looking as it should in no time."

Trust Sheila to manage to insult, threaten and bully me in one measly sentence. I thought about telling her to talk to her son about Lily, but really, why bother? Sheila had made up her mind that she'd single-handedly saved us from a problem. Why not let her feel the satisfaction of being my savior one more time?

"I've worked with Lily in the past. She knows what she's doing. She's especially in tune with what your social circle likes."

My social circle? That was rich. George and I didn't have any couple friends. Furthermore, I doubted that most of the people at Time in a Bottle could afford to have Lily Grey decorate their home.

We were still standing in the doorway. Suddenly, it came to me that Sheila didn't *want* George to overhear her. When we first got married, George usually stood by and let his mother run over me. However, lately he'd taken to telling her to back off.

"Are you sure you wouldn't like to step inside and share your thoughts with George?" Taking a step inside my foyer as I spoke, I manage to project an air of total innocence, but both Sheila and I knew that I was outflanking her. If she wanted to badger me about Lily, she would have to do it in front of her son.

"I have other things to do."

"Oh, that's too bad. I'll tell him that we had this little chat."

"You do that." But she didn't turn to go. She simply stood there and glared at me.

There was an entire conversation that passed between us, one that took place without any words. Sure, Sheila could still intimidate me, but I was slowly learning to stand up to the woman. Yes, George would always be her loving son, but he was becoming a man with his own opinions and his own view of the world. Okay, we were not soulmates. Nor was our marriage a love match. But we were in it together, and somedays Sheila represented a threat to our happiness.

Days like today.

~

BLESS MAGGIE'S HEART. As I dropped off Anya, my friend assured me that she and her husband would both take tons of photos of Mathilda and my daughter. She'd also promised to take the girls to breakfast the next day.

I thanked my pal.

The Friday night crop was quiet this week, compared to the week before. I brought a bag of muffies from St. Louis Bread Co., and everyone enjoyed them. Bonnie and Vanessa were both there, so the three of us sat by each other. They gave me tutorials on the tools they used. I didn't get home until one in the morning.

When Anya came home Saturday, she talked a mile a minute about the dance and a cute boy named Justin. Sunday is family pancake day. George must have gotten my message because he stayed home all weekend. That was the first time in a long time that he'd been around for both Saturday and Sunday.

On Monday, George took Anya to school. I pulled into the parking lot at Time in a Bottle and realized the store no longer seemed foreign to me. Instead, it seemed like I belonged. Like I'd been coming here for ages.

"Hello, Sunshine!" Dodie's voice boomed from where she was standing at the back of Time in a Bottle. "Am I ever glad to see you."

Now that was a greeting that made my heart sing. I realized that I, too, was happy to see Dodie.

This time the scrapbook stock didn't seem overwhelming. Unlike my other visits, today I had an idea for what I was looking. The colorful pages that decorated the walls now made sense to me. I could enjoy the handiwork that created them, as well as the mix of colors, patterns and textures. I actually knew exactly what I wanted to buy and which tools I wanted to take for a test run.

As Dodie walked toward me, I only glanced at her. Mainly I kept staring at all the visual beauty around me. That's probably why I failed to notice that she was being followed by a man in a navy blue jacket and gray slacks. The expression on his face suggested he was not amused.

"Detective Rowe, this is Kiki Lowenstein. She's one of my newest scrapbookers."

The policeman extended his hand and shook mine firmly. "Good to meet you, Mrs. Lowenstein. Although I wish it was under other circumstances. Mrs. Goldfader here tells me that you were here the night that Eloise Silverman died. Did you notice anything suspicious about her behavior?"

"Could it have been an attempt at suicide?" The words were out of my mouth before I could stop them.

The piercing way he studied me made me glad that I'd worn my nicest pair of jeans and a cute white blouse. Most days, he might have mistaken me for a homeless person.

"Why do you ask?" he said.

I shrugged. "I've done a little reading about common after-effects of WLS, Weight Loss Surgery. I was surprised to see that there's a higher than average percentage of suicides among people who've had it. Eloise was candid about having problems. Her husband left her. Her daughter was moving away. Her friends deserted her."

"But she felt well enough to come to a scrapbook party, didn't she?" Detective Rowe watched my reaction carefully.

"Yes, sir. She did." I thought a minute. "Have you looked at what she was working on that evening? She was doing a lot of writing in a notebook."

"I haven't been through her things carefully. Not yet. Just gave them a cursory glance." He crossed his arms over his chest and rocked back on his heels. "There wasn't any drinking here that night, was there, Mrs. Goldfader?"

This was a test. Would Dodie tell him that I thought I'd smelled booze on Eloise's breath? Or would she omit that nasty little fact because it might make her look bad?

"I did not serve any alcohol, nor did I see Eloise drink anything that looked alcoholic," Dodie responded truthfully. "That said, Kiki and her friend Maggie Earhart have a different view of what happened."

I smiled to myself. Dodie had passed a test in my mind. She was honest even though the situation might bite her on the backside.

Detective Rowe turned to me. "Is that so, Mrs. Lowenstein?"

"As far as I know, Eloise didn't imbibe. At least, I didn't see her drink anything. But I smelled alcohol on Eloise's breath!"

"Here's the crazy part about that." Dodie sounded genuinely puzzled. "I gave Eloise an unopened bottle of water from my cooler."

"That's right." I nodded my head. "I saw Dodie fish around and grab the bottle. She actually pulled out two, and Eloise took one. I took the other. That's why it's so puzzling that I smelled alcohol on Eloise's breath. She didn't eat anything that might make that odor. I saw her eat a small quantity of the low-fat dip. Carrots. A couple of cucumber slices. Three oranges that she brought from home. That's all."

Funny how the mind works. Ideas are like those plastic pop beads I used have when I was a kid. One is attached to another. The phrase "low fat dip" spawned another phrase "recycle," and that reminded me—

"The water bottle."

"What?" Dodie raised an eyebrow.

"How many shots does someone take when they're injecting themselves with insulin?"

The cop and Dodie had baffled looks on their faces. "Who cares? What does that matter?"

I shook my head and tried to clear it. "How many diabetics were here at the crop on Monday? I know Mel is. Right before we ate, she got up and announced she was going to take her injection. Was there anyone else at the crop that you know was diabetic?

"No. Not that I know of." Dodie settled her hands on her hips and gave me a curious look. "Why?"

"I remember that Mel told you she put her syringe in a plastic bottle and tossed it in the trash. But when I went to the bathroom later, there were three syringes in a plastic bottle in the trash. That doesn't make any sense, does it?"

Detective Rowe lifted a shoulder and let it drop. "Why would that matter?"

"I don't know. It just seems odd. Surely Mel didn't inject herself twice. So why three needles?"

"It's probably nothing." I sighed. "But it sure seems weird, doesn't it?"

"Recycling goes out today." Dodie cast a glance at the back room. "Couldn't hurt to grab it and look at that water bottle more carefully."

The three of us hurried into the back room. A grinding of gears and a rumble greeted us. Dodie threw open the back door in time for us to watch the recycling truck drive away. I hung back, not wanting to be in the way. But there was no mistaking the blue and white colors that signaled the truck's purpose.

Detective Rowe practically flew off the back stoop. The top of his head barely visible from where I stood.

"Too late," he said, as he rejoined us.

"Oh, well. It was a dumb idea," I admitted.

We moved back onto the sales floor and took seats around the craft table.

The cop pulled a notepad out of his back pocket. "Can I have your full name again? And your address, Mrs. Lowenstein?"

I gave him my details.

"In your opinion, Mrs. Lowenstein, could one of Mrs. Silverman's friends slipped her an alcoholic beverage without her realizing it? Could someone have tried to kill her?" His question came like a slap in the face.

Kill her? Could someone at our crop actually be a murderer?

"I don't know." I rubbed my arms. Goosebumps stood at attention on my flesh. "The others were angry with her. Spiteful. They went on and on about how much money she'd spent on weight loss surgeries."

Dodie shook her head. "I stayed out of it, but I couldn't help overhearing everything. Here's the deal: Eloise's father died of a heart attack. He lingered a few days after the initial attack. Long enough to tell her that he didn't want her to die like he had. He, too, was morbidly obese. He urged her to use the money she'd get from his life insurance policy and have weight loss surgery."

I didn't understand. "But the others kept teasing her? It was *her* money, right?"

Dodie smiled at me. "You'd think spending it would be up to her, wouldn't you? And you'd think that her father's wishes would count. But there's more to the story."

"Care to explain?" Detective Rowe urged her. He'd jotted a few words on the green paper in front of him.

"Eloise told me that after her dad died, her husband, Harvey, got it into his head that they should use the money to buy a house they'd seen for sale down in Lake of the Ozarks. Harvey Silverman's timing was really bad. He brought up the idea in front of the other couples. They liked that. The men were all big fishing buddies. The wives thought it would be fun. They assumed that the Silvermans would let them use the house whenever they wanted. I guess everyone was chattering excitedly when Eloise put her foot down and said it was her money and she was using it for weight loss surgery. That's why everyone got upset with her. They felt like Eloise kept them from all having a lake house they could enjoy."

"Huh." Detective Rowe chuckled. His shoulders relaxed, and he shoved his notebook deeply into his pants back pocket.

I rubbed my eyes and stared off into the distance. "That doesn't make sense. It was *her* money. Hers to do with as she wished. Her father specifically given it to her, and even directed her to have the surgery! Where on earth did they get that sense of entitlement?"

"True." Dodie heaved a long low sigh. "You're still young, Sunshine. As you get older, you'll see that people can develop a weird sense of privilege. Especially friends who get close and who don't understand boundaries. All those couples that Eloise and Harvey ran around with felt like they were sharing what little they had. Then up pops Eloise with a windfall, and they figured what was her was theirs. They were eager to help her spend her inheritance."

Detective Rowe chuckled. "I've seen that in my corner of the world, too. I had a buddy on the force who won a nice chunk of change in the lottery. He and his wife were thick with this other couple. After he won, he decided that he and the missus should finally go on a honeymoon, alone. Just the two of them. Booked a trip to the Bahamas. The buddy and his wife were furious. They went on and on about how if they had won the money they would have shared it with other people. Needless to say, it caused a big rift in the department."

"Wow." That was all I could think of to say.

"Can I get either of you a bottle of water?" Dodie asked.

Just like that, I had a flash of insight. "Dodie, that water bottle we were looking for wasn't in the recycling! It was in the trash. The small plastic can in the bathroom. You couldn't recycle a bottle with dirty needles inside it."

The three of us stared at each other like a weird Monty Python sketch. None of us were particularly thrilled about pawing through Dodie's trash, but hey, what else could we do?

"I'll get a big black trash bag," Dodie said as she moved toward one of her tall metal shelf units. "That way we can dump the contents of the plastic trash can in a pile."

"I suppose you could sit this one out." I thought about all the personal stuff in my own trashcans at home and cringed.

"I've got three daughters. Besides, if you find that bottle, I need to be able to testify that I actually saw it pulled out of the pile." With a short hoot of a laugh, he added, "On TV cops pull their guns. In real life, digging through trash is more realistic. Of course, if you tell anyone my secret, I'll have to kill you."

I liked Detective Rowe a lot more after his quick retort. He was more human, I guess. Humor can do that. Victor Borge once said that laughter is the shortest distance between two people. He was right.

Dodie scrounged up three pairs of latex gloves. Thus appareled, she and I stood to one side as Detective Rowe upended the trash can.

We got lucky. The plastic bottle magically rolled out and onto the floor in front of Dodie's feet. Detective Rowe grabbed it and held it to the light. Sure enough, there were three syringes rattling around inside.

## 11
---

*A*fter the detective left with the plastic bottle, I brought my supplies to the front counter for Dodie to ring up.

She concentrated, making sure she correctly plugged in all the prices. Then she moved to paper and pencil to calculate a healthy discount.

"You don't have to do that," I protested.

"You're right. I don't. But seeing as how you might have saved me a bundle in legal fees, I think I owe it to you, don't you? You showed up just in time to tell the good detective that I didn't serve any alcohol."

I laughed. "Is that your idea of twisting my arm?"

"Sort of." She laughed, too. "How's it working?"

"Pretty good," I said. "Dodie, do you really think those extra needles are the answer?"

"I have no idea, but their presence doesn't make sense, does it? I read a lot of mysteries. When there's an object out of place, that's a clue. I can't help but hope those syringes will tell Detective Rowe what really happened to Eloise."

Dodie leaned across the counter. "Look. I know you think I'm blowing smoke up your skirt. I know you've decided that I'm being complimentary because I want to keep you as a customer. But that's not the case. Sure, I'd love for you to keeping coming back. I'd be stupid not to want you. However, I sincerely meant it when I told you that you've got a real knack for this. Scout's honor." With that she performed a crooked three-finger salute. "You're not just good at this, Kiki. You're amazing."

"That's really nice to hear. Until now I've only ever been good at getting pregnant. By accident."

Dodie gave me a lazy grin. "So I've heard. Sheila has mentioned it several times."

"Terrific." I signed the receipt. "I bet she's given you an earful. I'm the *shiksa* who came to dinner and overstayed her welcome. A blight on humanity. A temptress out to destroy the Jewish race."

"Actually, Sheila says you're a good mother. She adores her granddaughter. Sure, she wishes you were Jewish, but she realizes that's not the only determinant of a person's value."

"Does she really?" I raised an eyebrow to that.

"I've known her for years. All of us at temple take Sheila with a healthy dose of salt. You haven't been coming long enough for people to speak to you frankly. We all know that Sheila's been a princess her whole life. She's a world-class whiner. If you can get past that, she's not so bad. Not really. Wait until she hears what a natural you are at scrapbooking."

"Right. I'm sure she'll be tickled pink." My voice fairly dripped with sarcasm.

"Sheila puts family first. Trust me on that. When she hears that she has something to brag about, she'll be your biggest cheerleader." Dodie handed over my purchases. "Not that it matters."

"Not that it matters?" I repeated like a parrot, but I wasn't sure what Dodie meant.

"Her opinion doesn't matter. Not to me. And it shouldn't matter to you. What matters is what you think of yourself."

"Hmm." And on that note, I said, "Thank you," and walked out of the store.

What *did I* think of myself? I wondered.

Dodie had posed a good question, a very good question, indeed.

RATHER THAN BRING her idea boards back to the house, Lily dropped them off at George's office. He brought them home.

I wasn't much impressed. Lily was a fan of gilt and glitz. She'd suggested that our powder room off the foyer be wallpapered in a black background with pink roses. The paper clocked in at an overpriced $125 per roll.

She'd proposed that our master bedroom should look like a boudoir directly out of *Arabian Nights* with a black paisley satin bedspread trimmed in gold. The walls of the room were to be painted a golden yellow, and the dark walnut furniture she chose had a distinctively French flair.

"Everyone at the office loved the master bedroom. Our secretary couldn't get over how romantic it was," George said.

"Uh-huh." I couldn't get over the master bedroom either. I wondered where we'd find a snake charmer to play his flute while coaxing a snake out of a basket.

As for the $125 a roll wallpaper, I thought it totally excessive. Over the top.

I didn't like the big roosters and the gaudy yellow and dark green trim she proposed for the kitchen. Nor was I fond of the very masculine brown leather sectional she wanted for the great room. We did a lot of sitting in there as a family. I knew that the leather would stick to the back of our legs in warm weather. The huge brown piece would take up a lot of room and completely dominate the space. Lily's proposed cowhide rugs seemed puny by comparison. I almost expected her to hang a pair of spurs over the mantelpiece.

In the end, I threw up my hands. It was either that or throw up my lunch. Maybe Lily's ideas would look better in person than on flimsy sheets of foam core board.

I lobbied for a long folding table that I could set up in the basement. That would be my crafting area. George and I agreed that I needed a good chair, a filing cabinet, shelves, and a good overhead light. Other than that, I was more than willing to surrender the rest of the house to Lily, with one other exception. She was to leave the guest bedroom and adjoining bathroom alone. Those were actually my rooms, since George and I didn't occupy the same bedroom.

As long as I had places to escape to, I didn't care what Lily did.

Over the course of the coming weeks, painters and wallpaper hangers moved around me while I concentrated on putting scrapbook pages together. Inside my albums, I could combine colors to my heart's content.

One day I realized that the paint being used on our walls was essentially the same stuff that Dodie sold at the scrapbook store in smaller containers. Using a plastic spoon, I scooped up enough to fill empty film canisters with black, white, gold, rose, blue, and gray to name a few.

Playing with the paints brought me no end of enjoyment, as did adding small oddments of wallpaper to my albums.

Because the master bedroom is huge, it took two days to paint it. The workers finished on a Friday. They hauled their tall ladder out of the master bedroom right about the time that George pulled up in the driveway, bringing Anya home from school.

My husband and daughter hurried up the stairs to greet me. I was standing outside the master bedroom, debating whether to look inside.

"Have you seen it?" George was breathless with excitement as they reached the landing.

"No, I haven't. They kept the door closed. Shall we look together? Anya? Care to do the honors?"

"Sure. On the count of three. One, two, three!" With that, she flung open the double doors.

George and I gasped in unison. The gold shade that Lily had chosen looked exactly like the mess Anya used to leave in a poopy diaper after eating a jar of squash baby food. There are no words to describe how bad the place looked. The gold Lily had chosen reflected a slightly green tint, turning it sickly. The sight of it on all four walls was nothing short of disgusting.

George muttered a string of curse words.

Anya got a fit of the giggles. "This is awful. It's so ugly. Who picked it?"

I could only spit out one word: "Ghastly."

"This is horrible. Terrible." George shook his head mournfully. "And to think it cost me nearly a thousand dollars between the paint and the labor. I've seen mistakes before, but this one takes the cake."

"Cake? I think it looks like an explosion inside a mustard jar." I pinched my nose. "What's more, the stink of the paint is making me woozy. Anyone else feel sick?"

Anya nodded. "Yes, but for other reasons. I've never seen anything this gross."

"I have," George said, "but I flushed it down a toilet."

That set us all giggling.

Lily might not be a success as a designer, but she sure was a world champion comedian.

THE DAY after we viewed Lily's disgusting color choice for the master bedroom, George called her and asked her to come by his office. As he described the scene to me, she pranced in with a terribly self-satisfied look on her face.

"See this?" George asked after she'd taken a seat. "It's the color sample you chose for our bedroom."

"Uh-huh." Lily practically preened.

"Never, ever suggest it to any of my clients," George said as he solemnly ripped the color sample to shreds. "This is without a doubt the most disgusting, gross excuse for a color that I've ever seen. I can't even describe to you how horrible it is to wake up in a bedroom with this on the walls. It turns my stomach."

According to George, Lily got very defensive. She countered that golden-yellow was really hot right now. George said, "I don't care if it's hot or not. I don't care if it's the shade of the year. I have never in my life seen anything more nauseating on a wall. Ever. Please schedule your painters to come back to my house as soon as possible. I'd like for them to paint the bedroom this color."

He tossed her a new paint sample with one of the shades circled.

"Gray?"

"That's right. Kiki picked it, and I heartily approve."

THAT SAME DAY, I dropped by Time in a Bottle to pick up more adhesives. I was putting a couple of new tape runners in my shopping basket when Dodie spotted me and waved hello.

"Did the detective come back?"

"No." She leaned close. "But I did get a call from him. Let's go in the back room to talk."

Once we were away from the sales floor, I realized we might not know if customers arrived.

"There's a door minder," Dodie reminded me. "It dings when people come in."

She gestured for me to take a folding chair. "Soft drink?"

I asked for a Diet Dr Pepper. She handed me a can and grabbed a Sprite for herself. With a flick of the wrist, she opened up a second folding chair and sat down on it.

After a long gulp of her cola, Dodie said, "I have a friend who works at the police station. He tells me that they found a controlled substance in Eloise's bloodstream. Along with the alcohol they reported. Detective Rowe hadn't mentioned that to either of us. I guess he was holding back. Turns out, there were trace amounts of codeine in one of the needles. Not much but enough. And alcohol in all three needles."

"What?" I nearly jumped out of my chair.

"Uh-huh. Seems that Mel doesn't have to take her insulin as often as she pretended. A couple of months ago, Mel had bronchitis. Her doctor gave her a prescription for cough syrup with codeine in it. When she came to the crop, she brought along two syringes with alcohol and one with a mix of booze and codeine."

"But why? And what did she do with them?"

"Mel injected the contents of the syringes into Eloise's oranges. Remember? Mel knocked them off the table and then volunteered to wash them?"

"So you're thinking Mel did all that on purpose?" I swallowed. "That's so...premeditated. And evil."

Dodie spread her fingers wide. "WLS changes your metabolism dramatically. I guess it varies from person to person. Mel knew that. She'd looked into WLS for herself. She'd actually been signed up for the surgery, and then backed out at the last minute. So she knew that a syringe might have been enough to make Eloise totally incapable of driving. And three syringes? She made sure that Eloise was totally messed up."

Dodie's conjecture made sense.

"But Mel didn't mean to kill Eloise, did she?" I hated the idea that I'd been sitting next to a murderer.

"I don't think so. I believe Mel wanted to put a scare into her friend. Mel really missed Eloise as a friend. You see, she and Eloise were besties until the whole WLS thing happened. I know that Mel missed Eloise. A lot. She wanted Eloise to start riding to the store with them again, but Mel wasn't about to apologize to Eloise. Instead, she wanted Eloise to beg them— Mel, Karen, and Angie—for forgiveness. Mel wanted to humble Eloise. I have a hunch that Mel figured if Eloise had a fender-bender, she'd be willing to come to crops with her old friends. Even though they'd treated her so cruelly. They wanted to make her dependent on them."

I wiped a tear from my eye. Dodie reached under her desk and grabbed a generic box of tissues for me.

"Sad, isn't it? Eloise went through all that so she could live longer, and then she died at a comparatively young age," I said. "Mel wanted more time with Eloise. Instead, she wound up killing her."

"I wasn't wrong, was I? I did smell alcohol on Eloise's breath?"

"I think so. You were better attuned to the smell than the rest of us." Dodie frowned. "My source tells me that they have Mel in custody. They're questioning her. Now that they have the syringes, they'll probably get a confession."

After a long sigh, Dodie gave me a tentative smile. "On what have you been working? Still having fun with scrapbooking?"

I tossed my empty Diet Dr Pepper can into the recycling bin. Shoulder to shoulder, Dodie and I walked out of the back room.

Because the "baby baba yellow" bedroom had been too funny to pass up, I had memorialized the adventure on a scrapbook page. I'd even stood in the middle of the master bedroom and taken a panoramic photo of the four walls.

Not surprisingly, the smell of the fresh paint had been over-whelming.

I explained to Dodie about the gross color the designed had chosen for us. "The painters have come back. They're covering over the ugly color, but as you can imagine the whole house stinks of paint odor. It's given me a headache—and a great reason to come here and get away from the smell."

"Do you need an aspirin?"

"That would be great. Thank you." While she went into the back, I looked at a set of die cut punches that could be used to create letters.

But my mind wasn't really on the punches. Something that Dodie had said was sticking out like a hangnail. I couldn't shake off the feeling that she'd hit on an important topic. One that involved poor Eloise.

Dodie returned with a bottle of cold water and a red and white plastic bottle of Tylenol. She shook out two round pills. I washed them down with the water and said, "Thanks."

"You're welcome to hang around here as long as you want," Dodie said. "Keep away from those paint fumes."

Of course, I found spending time in the scrapbook store to be a pleasant experience. I loved looking at paper and the new foam stamps that Dodie was in the process of stocking. However, even as I was enjoying myself, a wave of sadness swept over me.

"I know I should forget about what happened to Eloise, but it's hard. Really hard."

"You got that right, Sunshine." Dodie wondered out loud. "How could one friend even do that to another?"

I sighed. "I don't know. I guess it's possible. Friendship is another kind of love, and when lovers quarrel, they can go from love to hatred pretty quickly."

"Maybe I should have stepped in and done more. Each time those women got together here at the store, their conversations became more heated. There was a lot of emotion simmering under the surface. Before Eloise lost the weight, they all got along. Later, it was like a nest of hornets all riled up. Instead of stinging a mutual enemy, they all swarmed around Eloise."

I shook my head. "Honestly, Dodie. What could you have done? You aren't a mind-reader. You couldn't foresee the future."

She hung her head. "I know, I know. But it still rankles."

I gave her a hug. "You'd be cold as a block of marble if it didn't."

ANYA AND GEORGE got a kick out of the "baby baba yellow" page I'd done. After I picked up the dinner dishes, I went upstairs to the master bedroom and admired the gray paint. The smell was still pretty obnoxious, but the color was soothing.

George appeared at my shoulder.

"I think you should move back in here, Kiki. After all, you picked the color."

I'd been thinking the same. Instead of answering, I gave him a hug. "It does look better, doesn't it?"

"Sure does."

Later that night after Anya went to bed, my husband and I snuggled on that stupid futon we'd had for more than a decade. We watched a movie together. Hope flowered inside me. Maybe we could make this marriage work. We really did get along. We agreed on how important Anya was. I liked George. He was a good man. I loved him for being Anya's father.

George had the remote in one hand, and we were on our feet when the news anchor said, "A woman is in police custody this evening after she admitted to giving Eloise Silverman a controlled substance that led Mrs. Silverman to crash her car into a concrete abutment. Police are withholding comment, except to confirm that Mrs. Silverman was, indeed, the victim of foul play."

I stood there spellbound. So Mel really did kill Eloise. Whether she'd done so intently or not, I'd have to wait to hear. While we'd all been scrapbooking, Mel had plotted and carried out a cold-blooded plan that had ended her friend's life.

"What's the matter?" George was looking at me. "Can I turn the TV off?"

A sense of helplessness swept over me. Poor Eloise! All she had wanted was a better life for herself. She'd given up so much in her quest to be healthy. How could it all have gone so wrong?

"Kiki?" George reached for my hand.

I couldn't do anything more for Eloise. Nothing. I'd been witness to a crime and hadn't even known it. I couldn't have guessed what Mel had in mind. Thankfully, I didn't even have a clue. In my naiveté, I hadn't even realized that a friend could pull such a senseless stunt. One that ultimately cost another woman her life. How was that even possible?

But I'd learned. I'd not only learned about scrapbooking, I'd learned a bigger lesson about human nature. I'd also learned to trust myself.

As a consequence, I'd spoken up and told the truth about what I had seen. Now the matter was in the capable hands of the local police.

"What's wrong?" George was looking at me curiously.

"Nothing." I shook my head to clear it.

"Nothing?"

"Nothing."

"Come on, then." He led me upstairs to the newly painted master bedroom.

### ~ *The End*~

Looking for another great read? Joanna has a series just for you!

**Kiki Lowenstein Mystery Series (Agatha Award Finalist)**
A character-driven, page-turning and humorous contemporary mystery series set in St. Louis.
*Kiki, the main character, is real hoot... Lots of fun characters, pets and murders! Can't wait to read the next one! – A Reader*

You'll find the entire series here: https://amzn.to/3Vo8wwj

Love, Die, Neighbor: The Prequel to the Kiki Lowenstein
Mystery Series
Paper, Scissors, Death: Book #1 in the Kiki Lowenstein
Mystery Series -- AGATHA AWARD FINALIST
Cut, Crop & Die: Book #2 in the Kiki Lowenstein Mystery
Series
Ink, Red, Dead: Book #3 in the Kiki Lowenstein Mystery
Series
Photo, Snap, Shot: Book #4 in the Kiki Lowenstein Mystery
Series
Make, Take, Murder: Book #5 in the Kiki Lowenstein Mystery
Series
Ready, Scrap, Shoot: Book #6 in the Kiki Lowenstein Mystery
Series
Picture, Perfect, Corpse: Book #7 in the Kiki Lowenstein
Mystery Series
Group, Photo, Grave: Book #8 in the Kiki Lowenstein Mystery
Series
Killer, Paper, Cut: Book #9 in the Kiki Lowenstein Mystery
Series
Handmade, Holiday, Homicide: Book #10 in the Kiki
Lowenstein Mystery Series
Shotgun, Wedding, Bells: Book #11 in the Kiki Lowenstein
Mystery Series
Glue, Baby, Gone: Book #12 in the Kiki Lowenstein Mystery
Series
Fatal, Family, Album: Book #13 in the Kiki Lowenstein
Mystery Series
Grand, Death, Auto: Book #14 in the Kiki Lowenstein Mystery
Series

Law, Fully, Dead: Book #15 in the Kiki Lowenstein Mystery Series

Fleece, Navi, Dead: Book #16 in the Kiki Lowenstein Mystery Series

Mask or Raid: Book #17 in the Kiki Lowenstein Mystery Series

**Cara Mia Delgatto Mystery Series**

A group of spunky women living in Florida rely on friendship and creativity to weather life's storms in this contemporary series. *(This book is) comfort food for the reader weary of the endless parade of users and losers.* –Amazon reader

**You'll find the entire series here:** https://amzn.to/3PwJl7I

Tear Down and Die: Book #1 in the Cara Mia Delgatto Mystery Series

Kicked to the Curb: Book #2 in the Cara Mia Delgatto Mystery Series

All Washed Up: Book #3 in the Cara Mia Delgatto Mystery Series

Cast Away: Book #4 in the Cara Mia Delgatto Mystery Series

Ruff Justice: A Cozy Mystery with Heart--full of friendship, family, and fur babies!

Sand Trapped: Book #6 in the Cara Mia Delgatto Mystery Series

Jingle Bells and Empty Shells: Book #7 in the Cara Mia Delgatto Mystery Series

Ship Wrecked: Book #8 in the Cara Mia Delgatto Mystery Series

Paint Can Kill: Book #9 in the Cara Mia Delgatto Mystery Series

## The Jane Eyre Chronicles (Winner Daphne du Maurier Award)

Set in 1830s England, this series continues the life of Charlotte Brontë's iconic character.
*A lovely sequel to a much beloved novel.* – A Reader

**You'll find the entire series here: https://amzn.to/4a4BrJT**

Death of a Schoolgirl: Book #1 in the Jane Eyre Chronicles
Death of a Dowager: Book #2 in the Jane Eyre Chronicles
Christmas at Ferndean Manor: Book #3 in The Jane Eyre Chronicles
Death of a Gentleman: Book #4 in the Jane Eyre Chronicles

## Sherlock Holmes Fantasy Thrillers
(written with CJ Lutton)

Set in 1850s, this series expands on the Sir Arthur Conan Doyle classic while adding a paranormal twist.
*A fantastic story worth reading.*—A Reader

**You'll find the entire series here: https://amzn.to/49CGLnR**

Sherlock Holmes and the Giant Sumatran Rat: Book #1 in the Confidential Files of Dr. John H. Watson
Sherlock Holmes and the Father of Lies: Book #2 in the Confidential Files of Dr. John H. Watson
Sherlock Holmes and the Nefarious Seafarers: Book #3 in the Confidential Files of Dr. John H. Watson
Sherlock Holmes and the Time Machine: Book #4 in the Confidential Files of Dr. John H. Watson

## Friday Night Mystery Club Series
Decatur, Illinois/1986. Five female friends struggle to thrive and

survive while working in a sexist world. If you liked Mary Tyler Moore, you'll love this series!

*A great read for any mystery lover.* – A Reader

**You'll find the entire series here: https://amzn.to/3wHgINL**

**The Friday Night Mystery Club: Book #1 in the Friday Night Mystery Club Series**
**Monday Morning Blues: Book 2 in the Friday Night Mystery Club Series**
**Tuesday Trash and Trouble: Book 3 in the Friday Night Mystery Club Series**
**Tuesday Trash and Trouble: Book 3 in the Friday Night Mystery Club Series**

**Tai Chi Mystery Series**
A woman of a certain age does her best to fit in when her husband's job moves them to Washington, DC. This series offers an insider's look at life inside the Beltway.

*This is one of those books that are hard to put down* – A Reader

**Rising Water: Book #1 in the Tai Chi Cozy Mystery Series**
https://amzn.to/3wGIvwv

**

Love Recipes and Crafts? So do we—and we have a free gift for you that's full of fun stuff. Go to https://dl.bookfunnel.com/fsu24mc5qi

# ABOUT THE AUTHOR

Joanna is a New York Times Bestselling, USA Today Bestselling, and Amazon Bestselling author as well as a woman prone to frequent bursts of crafting frenzy, leaving her with burns from her hot glue gun and paint on her clothes. And the mess? Let's not even go there.

Otherwise, Joanna's a productive author with more than 80 written projects to her credit. Her non-fiction work includes how to books, a college textbook for public speakers, and books of personal essays (think Chicken Soup for the Soul).

Currently, she writes six fiction series: The Kiki Lowenstein Mystery Series (Agatha Award Finalist, contemporary, St. Louis setting, crafting), the Cara Mia Delgatto Mystery Series (contemporary, Florida setting, DIY, and recycling), the Jane Eyre Chronicles (Daphne du Maurier Award Winner, 1830s England, based on Charlotte Brontë's classic), the Sherlock Holmes Fantasy Thrillers (late 1800s, based on Arthur Conan Doyle's books), the Tai Chi Mystery Series (featuring a mature female amateur sleuth!) and the Friday Night Mystery Series (set in Decatur, IL in 1986 with a spunky female heroine.)

A former TV talk show host, college teacher, and public relations specialist, Joanna was one of the early Chicken Soup for the Soul contributors. She won a Silver Anvil for her work on the original FarmAid concert to benefit farmers.

In her ongoing quest never to see snow again, Joanna lives with her husband and their Havanese puppy, Jax, on an island off the coast of Florida. You can email her at jcslan@joannaslan.com or visit her website at https://linktr.ee/jcslan

Join Joanna on Substack. She shares news on writing, crafting, book discounts, releases, contests, giveaways, and more! Go to–https://joannacampbellslan.substack.com/